THE MELODY LINGERS ON

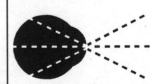

This Large Print Book carries the
Seal of Approval of N.A.V.H.

GALE
CENGAGE Learning·

LIBRARY OF CONGRESS CATALOGING-IN-PUBLICATION DATA

Clark, Mary Higgins.
    The melody lingers on / Mary Higgins Clark. — Large print edition.
        pages cm. — (Thorndike Press large print basic)
    ISBN 978-1-4104-7850-4 (hardback) — ISBN 1-4104-7850-5 (hardcover)
    1. Large type books. I. Title.
PS3553.L287M45 2015b
813'.54—dc23   2015016815

Published in 2015 by arrangement with Simon & Schuster, Inc.

Printed in the United States of America
1 2 3 4 5 6 7 19 18 17 16 15

THE MELODY LINGERS ON

MARY HIGGINS CLARK

THORNDIKE PRESS

A part of Gale, Cengage Learning

Farmington Hills, Mich • San Francisco • New York • Waterville, Maine
Meriden, Conn • Mason, Ohio • Chicago

ACKNOWLEDGMENTS

Once again the tale has been told. In this case the song has ended.

As always I've enjoyed the journey. While I am happy to write the words "The End," there is also a certain poignancy about it. I have become very fond of the characters in this book. I leave you to discover anyone I am not fond of.

As usual there are those who walked the mile with me. To them a tip of the hat and my great gratitude.

First, of course, my editor of fifty years, Michael Korda. I am so blessed to have teamed up with him all these years.

Marysue Rucci, V.P., editor-in-chief at Simon & Schuster, for her wise input and guidance.

Elizabeth Breeden, for her diligence and patience throughout the editing process.

Art Director Jackie Seow, for the compelling cover art she creates.

Ed Boran, retired FBI agent and current president of the Marine Corps Law Enforcement Foundation, who was my mentor as I learned how the Bureau would investigate a crime like this one.

Interior Designer Eve Ardia, who instructed me on how to spend five million dollars decorating an apartment in this story.

Nadine Petry, my assistant and right hand these past seventeen years.

Rick Kimball, for his advice on how to move large amounts of money around — away from watchful eyes.

Finally my family support group — Spouse Extraordinaire John Conheeney for his unwavering support; my children, all of whom are always available and helpful when I want their comments on a chapter or two. They are especially helpful when they point out that an expression I am using is unrecognizable by today's generation.

Tempus fugit and all that!

Happy reading, one and all.

Mary Higgins Clark

In memory of June Crabtree
Dear friend since our days at
Villa Maria Academy
With love

1

Thirty-year-old Elaine Marsha Harmon walked briskly from her apartment on East Thirty-Second Street in Manhattan to her job as an assistant interior decorator fifteen blocks away in the Flatiron Building at Twenty-Third Street and Fifth Avenue in Manhattan. Her coat was warm but she had not worn gloves. There was a distinct chill this early November morning.

She had twisted her long auburn hair and fastened it at the back of her head. Now only wisps of it blew around her face. Tall, like her father, and slender, like her mother, she had realized after graduating from college that the life of a teacher was not the way for her to go. Instead, she enrolled in the Fashion Institute of Technology and after receiving a degree had been hired by Glady Harper, the doyenne of interior decorating among the wealthy and the socially ambitious.

Elaine always joked that she had been named after her paternal great-aunt, a childless widow who was considered extremely well-to-do. The problem was that Auntie Elaine Marsha, an animal lover, had left most of her money to various animal shelters and very little to her relatives.

As Lane explained it, "Elaine is a very nice name and so is Marsha, but I never felt like Elaine Marsha." As a child she had unintentionally solved that problem by mispronouncing her name as "Lane," and it had stuck.

For some reason she was thinking about that as she walked from Second Avenue to Fifth and then down to Twenty-Third Street. I feel good, she thought. I love being here, right now, at this moment, in this place. I love New York. I don't think I could ever live anyplace else. At least I wouldn't want to. But she probably would decide to move to the suburbs soon. Katie would start kindergarten next September, and the private schools in Manhattan were too pricey for her.

That reflection brought a familiar stab of pain. Oh, Ken, she thought. If only you had lived. Pushing back the memory, she opened the door of the Flatiron Building and took the elevator to the fourth floor.

Although it was only twenty of nine, Glady Harper was already there, as she had expected. The other employees, the receptionist and the bookkeeper, usually arrived by two minutes of nine. Glady did not forgive lateness.

Lane stopped at the door of Glady's private office. "Hi, Glady."

Glady looked up. As usual her steel-gray hair looked as though she had not taken the trouble to brush it. Her wiry figure was clothed in a black sweater and slacks. Lane knew that Glady had a closet full of exactly the same outfits and that her passion for color and texture and design was reserved exclusively for the interiors of homes and offices. Sixty years old, divorced for twenty years, she was called "Glady" by her friends and employees. One of her fabric suppliers had joked "glad-she's-not" would have been a more appropriate nickname, a remark that cost him a lucrative contract.

Glady did not waste time on greeting her. "Come in, Lane," she said. "I want to talk something over with you."

What did I do wrong? Lane asked herself as, following the command, she walked into the office and settled in one of the antique Windsor chairs in front of Glady's desk.

"I've had a request from a new client, or

11

maybe I should say an old client, and I'm not sure if I want to get involved."

Lane raised her eyebrows. "Glady, you always say that if you sense a client is going to be difficult, the job isn't worth it." Not that *you're* not difficult, she added silently. The first thing Glady did when she took on a client was to go through the home with a cart and ruthlessly get rid of any object she considered to be junk.

"This one is different," Glady said, troubled. "Ten years ago, I did the interior design on a mansion in Greenwich when Parker Bennett bought it."

"Parker Bennett!" Lane thought of the headlines about the fund manager who had cheated his clients out of billions of dollars. He had disappeared from his sailboat just before the theft was discovered. It was believed he had committed suicide, even though his body had never been found.

"Well, it's not quite him I'm talking about," Glady said. "The Bennetts' son, Eric, called me. The government has clawed back every penny it can from whatever Parker Bennett had. Now the house is being sold. What's left in there has no real value and they're going to let Bennett's wife, Anne, take out enough to furnish a condominium. Eric said his mother is absolutely indifferent to everything and he'd like me to do it for him."

"Can he afford to pay you?"

"He was very up-front. He said he had read that the biggest commission I ever received was from his father's 'spare no expense' instructions to me. He's asking me to do it gratis."

"And will you?"

"What would you do, Lane?"

Lane hesitated, then decided not to be ambivalent. "I've seen pictures of that poor woman, Anne Bennett. She looks at least twenty years older than she did in the society columns before the fraud was discovered. If I were you, I'd do it."

Harper pressed her lips together and looked up at the ceiling. It was a typical reaction when she was concentrating, whether it was over the exact shade of the fringe on a drapery or a decision like this. "I think you're right," she said. "And it certainly won't take too long to put together enough furniture for a condominium. I understand that it's in a town house development in Montclair, New Jersey. That's not that far from the George Washington Bridge, maybe forty minutes in all. At least there won't be too much travel time."

She ripped off a page from the pad and

pushed it across the desk to Lane. "Here is Eric Bennett's phone number. I gather some small investment adviser gave him a behind-the-scenes job. He had been doing very well at Morgan Stanley, but he resigned after they found out what Daddy Dearest had been up to. Make an appointment with him."

Lane carried the page to her own office, sat behind her desk, and began to dial the number on it. A firm, modulated voice answered on the first ring.

"Eric Bennett," he said.

2

A week later Lane and Glady drove up the Merritt Parkway to the exit marked Round Hill Road, one of the most exclusive areas in exclusive Greenwich, Connecticut. Route 95 would have been faster, but Glady enjoyed looking at the mansions. Lane was driving Glady's Mercedes. Glady had decided that Lane's Mini Cooper was too unassuming to park at the Bennett mansion.

Glady had been silent for most of the trip, a silence Lane had learned to appreciate. When her boss was ready to start a conversation, she would do it in her own time. In her mind, Lane, a lifetime admirer of Queen Elizabeth, compared it with what she had heard about the queen. You did not address her until she opened the conversation.

It was when they made the turn at the exit that Glady said, "I remember when I first came up here. Parker Bennett had bought that enormous house. The man who built it went broke before he could move in. The way it was designed it was the quintessence of bad taste. I brought in an architect, and between us we remodeled the interior. My God, they had a counter shaped like a sarcophagus in the kitchen. In the dining room they had painted their version of the Sistine Chapel. It was an insult to Michelangelo."

"If you were making architectural changes as well as doing the interior decorating, it must have cost a fortune," Lane said.

"It cost a king's ransom, but Parker Bennett didn't mind. Why should he have cared? He was spending other people's money."

The Bennett estate was on Long Island Sound. The massive red brick house with white trim could be seen from the road. As they turned into the driveway Lane noticed that the shrubbery had not been trimmed and the lawn was littered with dead leaves.

Obviously Glady had observed the same thing. "I imagine the landscaper was among the first to go," she commented dryly.

Lane parked in the curving driveway. Together they walked up the few steps to the massive oak door. It was opened as soon as Lane touched the bell.

"Thank you for coming," Eric Bennett said.

While Glady acknowledged the greeting, Lane scrutinized Eric Bennett. The man whose voice had impressed her was medium height and build. With the four-inch heels she was wearing, he was just about her height. He had a full head of graying blond hair and hazel eyes. She had researched everything she could find about the Bennett case and she realized that Eric Bennett was a younger version of his father, the courtly, handsome man who had cheated people out of their life savings.

Glady was introducing them. "My assistant, Lane Harmon."

"Eric Bennett, but you probably guessed that." There was irony in his tone and his smile was brief.

As was her custom, Glady came straight to the point. "Is your mother here, Eric?"

"Yes. She'll be down in a minute or two. She's with the hairdresser now."

Lane remembered that Anne Bennett was no longer welcome in the salon where she had been a longtime client. Too many of the other clients bitterly resented her because their families had been victims of Parker Bennett's greed.

The large foyer had a desolate appearance. The matching rounded staircases led to a balcony that could have accommodated an orchestra. Holes in the walls of the foyer were visible.

"I see the tapestries are gone," Glady observed.

"Oh, indeed they are, and they increased in value by twenty percent in the years we had them. The appraiser was delighted as well by the paintings you had my father purchase. You have a good eye, Glady."

"Of course I do. I had a virtual walk-through of the town house you bought for your mother in New Jersey, Eric. It's not bad at all. We can make it quite charming."

It was obvious to Lane that Glady had developed a friendly relationship with Eric Bennett in the year or so she had spent working at the mansion. Now in her usual brisk way Glady began to walk around the first floor.

The high-ceilinged room to the left had obviously been what most people call the living room, but Glady referred to it as "the salon." Graceful arched windows looked over the back acres of the property. In the distance Lane could see a pool house that was a miniature duplicate of the mansion and a covered swimming pool. I'll bet that's

Olympic sized, she thought. And I'll bet anything it's a saltwater pool.

"I see they took every stick of antique and custom-made furniture out of here," Glady said tartly.

"Another tribute to your good taste, Glady." This time Lane thought she was hearing a note of bitterness in Bennett's tone.

Glady did not respond to the implied compliment. "Anyhow, the furniture in the small den will be much more suitable for the new town house. Let's look at that room."

They passed the baronial dining room. Like the salon it was devoid of furniture. As they walked to the back of the house, Lane could see the room that had obviously been the library. Mahogany bookshelves were the only thing in it. "I remember your father's collection of rare books," Glady observed.

"Yes, and he started collecting them long before he opened his own investment fund, but that didn't seem to matter to the government." This time Bennett's tone was again noncommittal. "Frankly when I read a book I want to hold it and not worry that I might in some way damage the gilt-edged pages or the illustrations in it." He looked at Lane. "Do you agree?"

"Absolutely," Lane said emphatically.

Glady had shown her the pictures of the rooms in this mansion after she had completed the interior design. Each room had been exquisitely furnished in its own color scheme, with the overall effect both charming and warm.

But there was nothing either charming or warm about this house now. It had a neglected, even desolate feeling about it. The shelves of the bookcases had a thin layer of dust on them.

But then they continued walking further toward the back of the house. To the left there was a cheerful den still furnished with a comfortable couch and chairs, a round glass-topped coffee table, and matching mahogany drop-leaf side tables. Flowered draperies coordinated with the fabrics on the upholstery. Framed Monet prints on the walls and a carpet in a soft green shade completed the inviting effect.

"This was the staff sitting room, Lane," Eric Bennett observed. "It has its own separate entrance into the kitchen. Until last year we had a household staff of six."

"It's the furniture that we're going to move into the new town house," Glady said. "It's even more attractive than I remember. It will be fine for that first-floor den. And

I've already decided that the furniture in your mother's sitting room upstairs will be perfect for the living room there. We'll take a queen-sized bed from one of the guest bedrooms. The one in the master suite is too big for the town house. We'll do the same thing for the other two bedrooms. According to my notes, the table and chairs and buffet in the breakfast room will take care of the dining room. Now, is your mother coming down or can we go upstairs?"

If there's one thing Glady is, it's decisive, Lane thought. I'm glad she's going upstairs. I was beginning to think she'd work from the pictures. I'd love to get a look at the rest of the rooms.

"I think I hear my mother coming down the stairs," Bennett said. Abruptly he turned around. Glady and Lane followed him back to the front of the house.

Lane had found pictures of Anne Nelson Bennett on the Internet when she Googled her name. But the stunning blond socialite whose favorite designer was Oscar de la Renta was almost unrecognizable. Painfully thin and with a tremor in her hand, she was hesitant as she addressed Glady. "Ms. Harper, how nice of you to come. A bit different now than it was when you last were here."

"Mrs. Bennett, I know how difficult everything has been for you."

"Thank you. And who is this lovely young lady?"

"My assistant, Lane Harmon."

Lane took the extended hand and immediately realized that Anne Bennett's grasp was weak, as though she had no strength in her fingers.

"Mrs. Bennett, I am going to do the best I can to make your new home attractive and comfortable. Shall we go upstairs and I'll point out the furniture I want to select for you?" Glady asked.

"Yes, of course. What they deemed could only bring a few dollars in an estate sale was left for me. Isn't that generous? Someone else stole that money. Isn't that right, Eric?"

"We will prove his innocence, Mother," Eric Bennett said heartily. "Now, let's go upstairs."

Forty minutes later, Glady and Lane were on their way back to Manhattan. Then Glady observed, "It's been almost two years since the scandal broke. That poor woman still looks as though she's reeling from shock. What did you think of that portrait of the big crook smiling so benevolently at the world? I understand the paint was barely dry on it before he disappeared."

"It's a very good painting."

"It should be. Stuart Cannon was the artist, and believe me, he doesn't come cheap. But at the art auction nobody bid on it and they let her keep it."

"Do you think that Parker Bennett was framed?"

"Nonsense."

"But isn't all of the five billion dollars absolutely unaccounted for?"

"Yes. God knows where Bennett managed to hide it. Not that it will do him any good. Certainly not if he's dead."

"If he is alive, do you think his wife or his son knows where he is?"

"I don't have any idea. But you can bet that even if they have access to the money, they'll never get to spend it. Every nickel they ever spend for the rest of their lives will be watched like a hawk by the government."

Lane did not answer. The traffic on the Merritt Parkway was getting heavier. She wanted Glady to think that she was concentrating on it.

She knew that Glady had been too busy

saying good-bye to Anne Bennett to notice that Eric Bennett had asked her to have dinner with him.

3

The day after their visit to the Bennett mansion, Glady unveiled her decisions in her usual modus operandi. After making her regal pronouncements about the selection of the furniture to take from the Bennett mansion, Glady left the everyday details for Lane to follow up on.

"We've seen the virtual inside of the town house in New Jersey," she said crisply, "but I want you to go over there and get the feel of the place. As I've told you, when I finished the decorating ten years ago, Anne Bennett said that her staff den was the most inviting room in the whole house. So placing that furniture into the den there will be comforting to her. I've picked paint chips for all the rooms, but let me know if you think the colors work. We may have to do some mixing to get the shade I want."

Amused, Lane thought that while Glady had been willing to make one trip to the

Bennett mansion, she was not about to spend any more of her pricey time on this project, especially when she was doing it on the house.

She also realized that working on the details of this project was going to be intensely interesting for her. Like everyone else, she had read every word in the media about Parker Bennett, starting with the headline that announced that five billion dollars had vanished from the assets of the revered Bennett Investment Fund. In addition to his wealthy clients, he had targeted investors who were mainly middle-class, hardworking small business people. That made the crime even more despicable. Elderly clients had been forced to sell their homes or retirement condos. Others whose income from the fund had been their only asset had no choice but to move back in with their children, where resentment of each other had fostered breaks in formerly tightly knit families. Four suicides had been linked to the financial disaster.

"What are you waiting for?" Glady demanded. "I need you to be back here by twelve o'clock. Countess Sylvie de la Marco called me last night. She used to be Sallie Chico from Staten Island before she befuddled that poor old count into marrying her. He died about three years ago. I guess the mourning period is over if there ever was one. Now she wants to completely redecorate her apartment. We're due over there at twelve-thirty. It will be a long session. I'll try to steer her away from what is her version of good taste. She reminded me that she will have had an early lunch, meaning she doesn't have any intention of feeding us. So on your way back, pick up a hamburger at the drive-through at a McDonald's and eat in the car."

Glady looked down at the paperwork on her desk. Lane knew that was the sign that she was supposed to be on her way to New Jersey. Do not pass go. Do not collect two hundred dollars, she thought as she left Glady's private office, remembering the instructions from her favorite childhood game, Monopoly. With rapid steps she walked through the still-darkened reception area and out into the hallway. She was the only one on the elevator to the lobby but when she got off it, the ground floor was filled with people on their way to work.

The receptionist at their office, Vivian Hall, was the first person on line for the elevator. Sixty-two years old, she had worked for Glady for ten years, a record for any of the employees. Perpetually planning to lose weight, she was a well-proportioned size fourteen with a cap of light brown hair.

She stepped aside to talk to Lane. "How's the dragon lady?" she asked.

"In typical form." Lane smiled. "I'm heading to New Jersey to look at Mrs. Bennett's new digs. I have to be back in time to go with her to Countess de la Marco's duplex."

"Good old Glady." Vivian shook her head. "In eight hours getting a ten-hour day out of you. But you look as though you're handling it just fine. Love that outfit. You look great in that shade of blue."

Ken had always liked to see her wear this color. A wave of sadness washed over Lane. His birthday would have been tomorrow. Thirty-six. It had been five years since a drunk driver had slammed their car on the Henry Hudson Parkway. The car tumbled off the road, rolling over and over until it finally stopped. Ken died instantly, his neck broken. They had been married only a year and she had been two months pregnant. Of course, the driver had no insurance.

Over and over again, when that sadness enveloped her, she thought of her four-year-old daughter, Katie, whom she might so easily have lost that terrible day.

These were her thoughts as she walked briskly to the parking garage.

Ten minutes later Lane was entering the Lincoln Tunnel on her way to New Jersey. Thirty minutes later she was driving into the town house complex in Montclair that was the future home of Anne Bennett. Pretty area, she thought as she drove through the winding streets until she turned onto Cedar Drive. Following the street numbers, she parked in front of number twenty-one. It was part of a cluster of similar facades. The exterior was gray stone and she noticed with approval the large front window. Glady had taken one of the keys to the unit yesterday and Lane fished it out of her pocket.

Before she could open the door, a man suddenly stepped out of the next-door unit. "Hello," he called as he walked rapidly past the shared driveway to where she was standing. "Are you the new owner?" he asked. "Because if so, we're going to be neighbors. I just bought here as well." He extended his hand. "Anthony Russo, but better known as Tony."

"Lane Harmon." As she acknowledged the greeting, Lane took in the appearance of this next-door neighbor. About six foot two, blue-green eyes, sandy hair and a warm smile. Even though it was November he had the deep tan of an outdoorsman. She judged him to be in his midthirties.

"I'm not the new owner," she told him. "I work for the interior designer who is decorating the house."

He smiled. "I could probably use her."

Not at her prices, unless you have big bucks, Lane thought.

"I won't keep you," he said. "Who *is* moving in here?"

"Our client's name is Bennett," Lane said. She had already turned the key in the lock. "I'd better get busy," she said. "Nice to have met you." Without waiting for his reply, she pushed open the door and closed it firmly behind her. Without knowing why, she locked it.

She had seen the virtual inside of the unit but now, being physically there, she was pleased to see that it was flooded with sunlight. Further down the entrance hall, there was a staircase to the second floor. The entrance to the kitchen and a breakfast room was on her right. Walking into the kitchen, she noticed that she could look directly across the driveway into the breakfast room of Tony Russo's apartment. He was standing there unpacking boxes that were stacked on the table.

Afraid that he might glance in her direction, she quickly looked away. The first thing

we buy for this place is a shade for that
window, she thought.

4

Ranger Cole sat at the bedside of his wife, Judy, holding her hand as she lay motionless, her eyes closed, oxygen tubes in her nostrils. He knew that the second stroke would take her soon. Much too soon. Judy was sixty-six years old. They were only six months apart in age. She was older and he always joked that he had married an older woman for her money.

They'd been married forty-six years. Kids of twenty so in love that when they went to Florida on a bus for their weeklong honeymoon it had felt like a limousine. They'd held hands all the way down. Neither one of them had gone to college. She worked as a sales clerk in Macy's and he had a job in construction.

Her mother didn't want her to marry me, he thought. In school I'd always been in trouble for having fights with other kids. Too quick to turn my hands into fists. A nasty temper. Her mother was right but Judy calmed me down. I never was mad at her, not for one single minute. If I started yelling, like about a driver who cut me off, she would order me to stop it. Tell me I was acting like a child.

To both of their regret they never had been blessed with kids.

Ranger reached over and with a gentle stroke ran his calloused fingertips across his wife's forehead. You were always smarter than me, he thought. You were the one who told me I'd be better off getting a job with the city, that jobs in construction came and went. You were the reason I got to be a repairman on the Long Island Rail Road. I worked from one end of the island to the other. You said it fitted my nickname. My father started calling me Ranger when I was a kid because I was always out of range of where I was supposed to be.

Judy always told him how handsome he was. That's a joke, he thought. He was a short, bulky guy with big ears and bushy eyebrows, even though he tried to keep them trimmed.

Judy. Judy. Judy.

Anger welled up in the depths of Ranger's being as he thought about why Judy had had the first stroke two years ago after they learned that the money they had invested in the Bennett Fund had disappeared. Two hundred and fifteen thousand dollars that they were going to use to buy a condo in Florida. Money they had saved so carefully over the years. The condo they had seen was a real buy. An old lady who owned it had died and her family wanted to get rid of it furnished.

Judy had loved the way it was decorated. "Much nicer than I would have figured out how to do it," she said. "We'll give away everything here in the apartment. It's not worth the expense of getting a U-Haul. Oh, Ranger, I'm so ready to give up my job and get down to Florida and be in the sun. What's nice is with no mortgage to pay and having both our pensions and social security, if we're careful we won't have to worry about money."

And at just that time the money in the Bennett Fund had disappeared, and that was the end of buying the condo. A few weeks later Judy had the first stroke and he had watched her exhausting herself trying to keep up with the exercises to try to strengthen her left arm and leg. She tried to keep him from hearing her crying at night but of course he heard her.

It was Parker Bennett's fault that their

lives had been destroyed. A lot of people didn't believe that he'd committed suicide by taking a dive off that fancy sailboat of his. Ranger didn't believe that that jerk had jumped in the water. In one of the newspapers after Bennett disappeared, Ranger had seen his picture; he was sitting behind an antique, rich-guy desk in his office. Bennett's way of offing himself would be to sit behind that desk all dressed up like he is in that picture and get drunk on some single-malt scotch, then shoot himself, Ranger thought.

Our money helped pay for that fancy office.

And Judy had been so depressed and so sick that she had given up. He knew that was why she'd had the second stroke yesterday.

He knew she was dying.

Don't die, Judy. Please don't die.

The heart monitor beside the bed began to go off. It was a loud shrieking sound. In just a few seconds doctors and nurses were rushing into the room. One of them began pounding on Judy's chest.

Ranger could see that the blip on the screen that had been showing the heartbeats was no longer there. Now it was moving in a straight line.

He stared straight ahead. I can't live without her, he thought numbly.

He felt a hand on his shoulder. "I'm so sorry, Mr. Cole," the doctor was saying. "There was nothing we could do to save her."

Ranger shook off the doctor's hand and shoved it aside. He fell to his knees beside the bed. Ignoring the tubes that were still in her arms and nostrils, he put his arms around Judy and held her close to him. Overwhelming grief vied with murderous anger. Anger won. Bennett was alive. He was sure of it. He didn't know how he was going to make him suffer but he would find a way.

"I will find a way, Judy," he said aloud. "I promise you, I will find a way."

5

In his office at the Federal Building in lower Manhattan FBI supervisor Rudy Schell listened as a victim of Parker Bennett talked to him about Bennett's supposed suicide. Unlike other victims, it was not rage that Sean Cunningham was exhibiting. It was with almost clinical detachment that he was making his case that if Bennett had committed suicide in that area of the Caribbean, his body would almost certainly have washed up on the beach of Tortola.

Cunningham had made an exhaustive chart showing the currents around the spot where Bennett's sailboat had crashed in Sharks Bay on the north end of Tortola.

"If he had committed suicide, his body should have surfaced around Rough Point," Cunningham was saying.

Schell looked sympathetically across his desk at the man who was head of the Association for the Victims of Parker Bennett.

A retired psychiatrist, Cunningham had recognized the devastating effect the loss was having on the investors. He had made it a personal crusade to reach out and try to help them to adjust their changed circumstances. He had a website and urged victims to share with each other their feelings of frustration, anger, and depression.

The response had been overwhelming. People who had been total strangers had become friends and had gotten together for meetings in their local areas.

Cunningham was thin, with white hair and rimless glasses. He looked every day of his seventy years, Schell thought, ten years older than when they had met two years ago.

In the course of the investigation they had become good friends. As some of the other victims reacted with numb disbelief, anger, and despair, Cunningham had remained calm. He had lost the million-dollar trust fund he had set up for his two grandchildren. In response to Schell's questions he had said, "My son has done very well. He can afford to educate his children. I am deprived only of my joy in leaving a gift that would have bought them their first houses."

In the past two years Cunningham had spent a major amount of his time counseling many of the victims who were having difficulty putting their lives back together. At this point in the investigation Schell could not tell the doctor that the FBI's nautical experts had already come to the same conclusion. Ninety-nine to one Parker Bennett was still alive.

They were on a first-name basis. "Rudy, are you humoring me or do you think his so-called suicide was staged?" Cunningham asked now.

Schell replied carefully. "Sean, there is always that possibility. And given the way Bennett managed to hide what he was doing from the accountants and the SEC, it's entirely possible that he was able to get away with staging his death." He paused. "At least he's gotten away with it so far."

"Did you hear that Judy Cole died this morning?" Cunningham asked.

"No, I didn't. How did Ranger react?"

"It's hard to tell. I called him. He was very quiet. He said that the second stroke left Judy so disabled that he knew she wouldn't want to live if she'd learned how bad it would be."

"That doesn't sound like Ranger Cole. When we interviewed him two years ago, he was like a man possessed. I think if he had bumped into Bennett at that point, he would have killed him with his bare hands."

"I'll keep in close touch with him." Cunningham stood up. "Shall I leave you the nautical charts I made? I have another copy."

Schell did not hint that the FBI charts were virtually identical to the ones Cunningham had prepared. "I definitely want them for the file. Thanks."

When Cunningham was gone, Rudy leaned back in his chair and, in a characteristic gesture, ran the palm of his hand along his cheek. He could feel the stubble that was already beginning to grow on his face. He smiled at the memory of his grandfather telling him that they used to call that stubble "five o'clock shadow."

I sure have it, he thought. It used to bother me but now I don't care. In fact it was a real plus when I needed to go undercover. He got up and stretched. It had been another disappointing day trying to follow the trail of the money Bennett had stolen.

But we will find him, he vowed, we will find him.

But even as he made that promise he wondered if he would be able to keep it. With the Bureau's focus on terrorism and the number of individuals who had to be watched, resources were stretched very thin.

The previous week an agent who had worked with him on the Bennett case had been reassigned. He did not have the heart to tell Cunningham and the investors that if a break in the case did not happen soon, more agents who were working with him would be assigned elsewhere.

6

Lane made it back from the Bennett town house barely in time to leave with Glady to meet the Countess de la Marco. Her apartment was on the corner of Fifth Avenue opposite the Metropolitan Museum of Art. The few blocks immediately surrounding the Met were known as Miracle Mile. "Isn't this considered one of the best addresses in New York?" Lane asked Glady as they got out of the cab.

"Yes, it is," Glady agreed. "But the fact is that the most important address in New York is Seven Forty East Seventy-Second Street. I've been in the triplex that was built for John D. Rockefeller there. It would take your breath away. But even more important, it's furnished tastefully. I couldn't have done a better job myself. Now, what are you standing here for? It's cold. Let's get inside."

Countess de la Marco turned out to be a stunning blonde with the figure of a Victoria's Secret model. "It's obvious she had a lot of work done," Glady murmured to Lane when, after they were invited to sit in the library, the countess excused herself to take a phone call. "She looks thirtyish. I know she's in her late forties and her hair is loaded with extensions. When she's in her sixties, her face will fall apart."

When the countess returned, she invited them on a tour of the apartment. For the next few minutes she treated them as visiting vendors but then became thoroughly intimidated by Glady. She ended up meekly agreeing to all of Glady's pronouncements about how the apartment should be refinished and refurnished.

After the tour they sat at a table in the den as Glady made sketches of the minor architectural changes she proposed to make throughout the apartment. At four o'clock Lane began to take stealthy glances at her watch. This could go on forever, she thought, and I have to be home by five thirty.

That was the time her wonderful babysitter, Bettina, insisted she had to leave. Finally, at twenty after four Glady stood up from the table. "I think that's enough for today," she said abruptly. "But let me assure you, Countess, that when I am finished you will have one of the most beautiful residences in New York."

"And to think that only six months before he died, my husband had the foresight to listen to me and withdraw his money from the Bennett Fund," the countess said unexpectedly. "If he had not, I assure you that I would not be redecorating this apartment."

Lane and Glady stared at her. "I didn't know you were involved in that fund," Glady said quietly.

"Oh, we were just two of the many," the countess said. As she spoke her brown eyes widened and her voice lost its modulated tone. "He had a dinner party for ten of us who were heavily invested with him. He toasted his wife. He couldn't have been more flowery in the way he spoke of her. But later I happened to pass the library on my way to the restroom. The door was open. He was on the phone. It was obvious that he was talking to a woman. He was telling her that before too long she would have everything she ever wanted. That was when I felt that if he could cheat on his wife after speaking so convincingly about how he cherished her, he might also be cheating in other ways."

"Did you tell the FBI about that conversation?" Lane asked.

"I did, but I got the impression that they knew he had had a lot of girlfriends over the years and whoever this one was, she was just one of many to whom he made lavish promises."

Lane knew there was a question she had to ask. "Do you think his son, Eric, was involved in the scam?"

Countess Sylvie remembered to speak in her carefully cultivated voice. "I haven't got the faintest idea," she sighed.

At four thirty, on the way down in the elevator, Lane asked, "Glady, something doesn't ring true to me. Do you think Parker Bennett would be so careless that he'd let someone overhear that kind of conversation?"

"Of course he didn't," Glady snapped. "The rumor always has been that Sylvie de la Marco, nee Sally Chico from Staten Island, was one of Bennett's girlfriends. This is her way of keeping the spotlight off herself. Who knows? Bennett may have given her a hot tip to get out of the fund while the getting was good."

7

As usual Katie was waiting at the door for Lane when she got home at ten after five. "Mommy! Mommy!"

Lane scooped her up and hugged her. "Who loves you?" she demanded.

Katie giggled. "You do."

"And who will love you forever and ever?"

"You will."

Lane ran her fingers through Katie's long golden-red hair. She got the hair from my genes, she thought. But those brilliant blue eyes are Ken's gift to her. As soon as she set her down, Katie tugged her by the hand. "I drew a new picture in school today," she announced proudly.

She had laid it out on the coffee table. Lane had expected to see a picture of one of the animals Katie loved to draw, but this one was different. It bore a remarkable resemblance to Lane in the jacket and scarf and slacks she had been wearing when they went to the Central Park Zoo last Saturday.

There was no question Katie had an extraordinary talent for drawing. Even the crayons she used vividly captured the colors Lane had been wearing that day.

Lane felt a lump form in her throat. As she showered praise on Katie, she could only think of how gifted an artist Ken had been; she almost said, "You sure are Daddy's girl," and then stopped herself. Be careful, she thought. As she gets older, she'll understand how talented he was.

Bettina, the nanny, had been with her since shortly after Katie was born. Small, with a compact body, with only a few strands of gray in her glossy black hair, Bettina at sixty-one had the energy of a woman half her age. For the last year she had been taking care of her elderly mother and needed to catch the six o'clock bus from the Port Authority to her home in New Jersey. Lane had been forced to give Glady an ultimatum. Either she left the office promptly at five or she would have to change jobs. Glady had reluctantly agreed, although she regularly muttered about how lucky Lane was to have such a kind and understanding employer.

A roast chicken and sweet potatoes were already in the oven. Asparagus was in a pan on the stove and the table in the dinette was set. Lane shed her coat and gloves and scarf and sat with Katie in their compact living room. It was their special time together. She always allowed the phone to take messages between the hours of five and seven. Her mother in Washington and her close friends understood that. It was a joke among them that the rule was made for the benefit of Glady, who thought nothing of calling Lane minutes after she arrived home. Sometimes they asked why Lane didn't change jobs. Lane's answer always was that Glady's bark was worse than her bite and it was deeply satisfying to work for someone who was so incredibly talented. "I learn something from her every day," she told them. "She not only is a marvelous designer but she can read people like a book. I wish I had that talent."

The phone rang twice during the time that she and Katie were having dinner but she did not check her messages until after Katie was tucked into bed at eight thirty.

Both of them were from Eric Bennett, asking her to have dinner with him on Saturday night.

She hesitated, put down her cell phone, then picked it up again. The image of the attractive man who, with a touch of irony in

his voice, had walked them through the Bennett mansion filled her mind.

Glady had said that she thought Eric might be innocent of any knowledge of the scam. "*Might* be innocent," not *is* innocent, Lane thought.

She hesitated, then pushed the call-back button on her cell phone.

8

"Were you talking to that nice young woman who was here with Glady Harper?" Anne Bennett asked her son. She had come into the former breakfast room just as he was ending his conversation. They were about to have their usual late dinner.

"Yes, I was," Eric said, smiling.

"I Googled her," Anne told him as she sat at the table and unfolded her napkin. "Thanks to you that's the one thing I've learned to do on the computer."

Eric knew that his mother had learned to use the Internet after the Fund failed because she wanted to see any news article that applied to his father. He had refused to teach her how to use Twitter because of the never-ending references to him. They came not only from the bitter investors who had lost all their money but also from comedians who had made Parker Bennett a source of their jokes. "Park your money with Bennett

and you'll never have to pay income tax again" was one of the latest.

He did not tell his mother that he had Googled Lane Harmon as well. "And what did you find out about her, Mother?" he asked.

"She has an interesting background," Anne said with a nervous gesture as she tucked a strand of hair behind her ear.

Watching her, Eric thought of how his mother's hair used to look. She had worn it in an elegant silver-tinted upsweep perfectly coiffed by Ralph, her longtime hairdresser. His blood boiled when he thought of how, after ten years as a valued customer and a generous tipper, she had been barred from returning to his salon. "Your presence will upset too many of our clients who lost money investing with your husband," he had explained.

His mother had returned home choking back tears. "Eric, he wasn't even apologetic," she had told him. Now a stylist from an inexpensive salon in Portchester came to the house once a week.

He opened the bottle of pinot noir that was in a Waterford crystal decanter next to his chair.

Marge O'Brian, their full-time housekeeper of fifteen years, was his father's staunchest defender and still came in to serve his mother lunch and dinner and to tidy up. One of the great problems of moving to New Jersey was giving up Marge, who could never leave her family in Connecticut.

Tonight he knew she had prepared a Waldorf salad, salmon, and wild rice, his mother's favorite dinner. He only hoped that when it came she would do more than pick at it.

Now he asked, "And what did you find out about Lane Harmon?"

"She was widowed in a car accident before her baby was born. She's the daughter of Gregory Harmon, the congressman who they said had the potential to be the next Jack Kennedy. He was killed in a crash when he went on a golf outing in a private plane with three of his friends. Lane was only seven years old. Isn't it terrible that she suffered that kind of loss twice?"

"Yes, it is." Eric reached for his mother's glass and filled it. "You may be pleased to know that I invited her to have dinner on Saturday night and she accepted."

Anne Bennett smiled, a genuine smile. "Oh, Eric, that's nice. She's so pretty and I can see how smart she is. She made me feel so comfortable. That Glady Harper may be doing us a favor, but she intimidates me."

"I suspect she intimidates everyone, Mother, even me," Eric joked.

Anne Bennett looked affectionately across the table at her son. Then her eyes filled with tears. "Oh, Eric, you're the image of your father. I so often think about how we met purely by happenstance. We were both going down the subway stairs. It was raining and the stairs were slippery. I slipped and almost fell. He was on the step in back of me. He grabbed me by my waist and held me against him and that was the beginning.

"He said to me, 'You are so pretty. Why do you look familiar?'

"I told him I had just started working as a secretary at the same firm where he worked. We went down the steps and he walked me to my train. A few days later he called and asked me out. That was it. When he proposed, he said that the moment he put his arms around me that day, he knew he would never let go of me again. I was dating someone else, but it didn't matter. He was history the day I met your father."

It isn't a blessing to be the image of my father, Eric thought. I can hardly go anywhere that people don't turn their heads and look at me. But what was more unsettling was that his mother repeated that story over and over again. His parents had been married eight years before he was born. His mother was now almost sixty-seven years old. He was beginning to wonder if she might be in the early stages of dementia.

Another problem, he thought.

"Do you want your coffee in the sitting room, Mrs. Bennett?" Marge asked as she began to clear the table.

The sitting room was the new name for the den that had been designated for the help.

"Yes we do," Eric answered.

"I'll have another glass of wine," Anne Bennett said.

Eric frowned. Lately his mother had been drinking too much wine. The house is dreary and desolate, he thought. It will be good when she moves to Montclair next week. Once Mother is settled there, I think her spirits will be much better.

He guided his mother by the arm as they walked down the hall. But when they went into the room he was startled to see that the music box his father had given to his mother long ago was on the mantel.

Anne Bennett reached up and took it down. "I love to hear it play. I know I told you it was the first present your father gave to me. It looks expensive but in those days it was only about thirty dollars. We both loved to dance. The figures dancing when the music plays are Czar Nicholas and Czarina Alexandra. But of course you know that."

No, I don't remember that, Eric thought. He did remember that the ornate little music box had been on his mother's dressing table for years. He had never been around when she played it.

As Marge brought in a tray with coffee, his mother lifted the lid of the box and the figures of the doomed couple began to dance.

"I don't know if you will recognize it," his mother said. "It's my favorite Irving Berlin song. It goes like this." She began to sing softly. " 'The song is ended but the melody lingers on.'

"Whether or not your father is alive or dead, our song is not ended and our melody lingers on," she said, her voice fierce and allowing no room for contradiction.

9

On Friday morning Lane made her usual stop at Glady's office and was surprised to see Glady poring over paint chips and swatches of materials.

She opened the conversation in her usual brusque manner. Holding up one of the chips, she said, "You're right. This deep blue is too dark for Anne Bennett's bedroom. But you're wrong about going to another color. The answer is to put white wainscoting at chair height on the walls. That will punch the blue and be very dramatic."

"And expensive," Lane reminded her. "Are you doing this without charge?"

"Of course not. I'll bury it in the bill I present to Countess La-di-da. She can afford it. I still say that bandit tipped her off to get her money out of his fund."

"I'll take care of it," Lane promised.

"Don't be in such a hurry. That's not all."

"Sorry."

Glady held up five swatches of material. "I don't like the spread and drapes we took from the old guest room at the Bennett mansion. I've ordered these. Spread, pillows, bed skirt, vanity skirt, draperies, and chaise lounge. It will make a beautiful bedroom for that poor woman."

"And all these to be charged to the countess?"

"Of course. We'll do a little claw back of our own."

Trying not to shake her head, Lane headed for her own office. This was the time when Glady called her suppliers and tortured them to be sure that there would be no delay in having work done or supplies delivered on time.

Lane knew it was a good opportunity to make a quick phone call to her mother. Mom will be in the shop by now, she thought. Her mother owned an antique shop in Georgetown. She was always trying to persuade Lane to move there, saying she would finance her opening a decorating business of her own.

Lane knew she was not ready to do that yet. Even just a minute ago I learned something from Glady, she thought. And besides that, I have no interest in living near my stepfather.

Her mother answered on the first ring. "Lane, I was about to call you. How's Katie?"

"Great. She's turning into quite a little artist."

"No surprise."

"And I'm fine too," she said.

Her mother laughed. "Believe it or not that was my next question," Alice Harmon said defensively.

Lane visualized the dynamic woman who was her mother. Alice Harmon Crowley was in her midfifties. Her once-auburn hair was now completely gray. She wore it in a short bob around her face. She had no use for having to fuss with it. "There are better things to do than stand in front of a mirror and primp yourself," was the way she put it. Tall and slender, she did yoga at six o'clock every morning.

She did not remarry for ten years after Lane's father died in the plane crash. Lane's stepfather, Dwight Crowley, wrote a daily political column for the *Washington Post* and was considered an important player on the Washington scene. He and her mother were married just as she was starting college. She was glad that her mother was happy with Dwight, but she didn't like him. His idea of a discussion was "I talk; you listen," she thought. He's nothing like Daddy.

Dwight and her mother were a sought-after couple in Washington's inner circle. Now Lane asked, "Have you been to the White House this week?"

"No, but we've been invited to a White House dinner for the Spanish ambassador next week. What have you been up to?"

"Glady got a call from Parker Bennett's son. We're doing work on Anne Bennett's town house in New Jersey."

"I know a dozen people who got caught in the Bennett mess," her mother said. "It's been horrible for them. Did you meet the son? A lot of people, and especially Dwight, think he was in on the scheme."

Lane had been about to say that she'd made a date to have dinner with Eric Bennett Saturday night, but the sudden, chilly tone in her mother's voice made her decide to say nothing about it. When the call ended she acknowledged to herself that it had been a mistake to accept Eric Bennett's invitation. Thanks to the extra work on the New Jersey town house, she would be in and out of it much more than she had anticipated. She knew that Eric worked behind the scenes in another broker-age firm and that he had an apartment in

Manhattan. But one of the bedrooms was being furnished for him. Glady had said that he had told her he planned to stay over regularly with his mother.

It isn't a good idea to have dinner with him, Lane thought, dismayed. Why didn't I tell him I was busy?

She did not like the answer that in all honesty she had to face. Eric Bennett was a very attractive man and she was looking forward to seeing him again.

The sins of the father should not be visited on the son, she thought firmly, and then turned her attention to the swatches that Glady had handed to her to decorate the bedroom of the woman whose husband had stolen five billion dollars.

Dr. Sean Cunningham sat beside Ranger Cole at the funeral service for his wife, Judy. It was being held in the chapel of the funeral parlor. Her body had been cremated and the urn containing her ashes was on a table covered with a white cloth in the aisle. Ranger had insisted that he carry the urn himself and place it on the table.

It was obvious to Cunningham that Ranger was not hearing one word of the service. His eyes were fixed on the urn, and when he suddenly burst out sobbing, his plaintive wail could be heard throughout the chapel.

There were about forty people there. Cunningham guessed them to be coworkers and neighbors but when the service was over and they went outside he recognized a number of people who, like Ranger, had been victims of Parker Bennett.

One of them, Charles Manning, a retired lawyer, seventy-eight years old, came up to Cunningham. Nodding his head toward Ranger, who was now clutching the urn, he said, "Sean, I think Ranger could go off the deep end. Is there anything you can do to help him?"

"I think he could too," Cunningham agreed. "I'm going to talk to him every day and see as much of him as I can. Denial and anger are the first steps in the grieving process. He's certainly in both stages right now."

"And what is the next step?"

"Depression. And finally, acceptance."

Together the men turned and looked directly at Ranger Cole. Stone-faced, he had begun to walk away from the friends who had tried to comfort him. Realizing it was useless, no one tried to stop him but watched as, hugging the urn to his body, he turned the corner and disappeared from their sight.

Acceptance? Sean Cunningham knew that there was no chance that that would happen to Ranger Cole. But where would he vent his anger?

Sean could not know that Ranger was seeking an answer to that question. His tears blinded him as he stumbled down the street. My Judy died before her time. A phrase from the Bible unexpectedly came into his mind. "An eye for an eye and a tooth for a tooth."

He knew what he was going to do.

10

FBI agent Jonathan Pierce, alias Tony Russo, had hired a moving van to deliver the furniture he had ordered for his new town house. He did not want the logo of the company from which he was renting the furniture to be seen by his new neighbors. As far as they know I'm newly divorced, no kids, about to open a new brasserie here in Montclair, he thought. That will give me an excuse to be in and out regularly.

And an opportunity to keep Anne and, to a lesser degree, Eric Bennett under scrutiny.

There was no doubt in Jon's mind that Eric Bennett was in on the fraud. How else would Parker Bennet have gotten away with it? Someone had to have been working with him.

In a final effort before the case went cold they had been granted warrants for court-authorized wiretaps for the phones and residences of Eric and Anne Bennett, as well as listening devices to record conversations outside their homes.

Jon had been placed by Rudy Schell as the next-door neighbor to Anne Bennett.

"It's possible they'll say something to each other that will give us an indication if the father's alive or if they're in on it. My guess is that Eric Bennett may be smart enough to have his mother's town house swept for bugs before she moves in next week. Wait a week or so and then go in and do a little bugging of your own."

11

On Saturday evening Katie sat cross-legged on Lane's bed as Lane dressed for her dinner with Eric.

"You look pretty, Mommy," she observed. "I like it when you wear that dress."

Lane had planned to wear a black pantsuit but at the last moment had changed into a dark green wool dress that she knew brought out the highlights in her auburn hair. She had bought it on sale in Bergdorf Goodman. Even on sale it had been pricey but she knew that it had the unmistakable combination of beautiful fabric and couture design.

Katie's comment made her pause as she snapped on the small diamond and emerald earrings that had been left to her by her grandmother. Why am I wearing this dress? she asked herself. It's just a casual dinner date.

Eric Bennett's image flashed in her mind.

She liked the hint of gray in his hair, the hint of irony in his expression, the hint of sadness in his voice when he talked about his father.

Katie's voice broke into her reverie. "I like those earrings too, Mommy."

Lane laughed. "Thank you, Katie." Daddy used to buy me play jewelry when I was Katie's age, she thought. I loved to wear it and I shared it with my dolls. He would sing that song to me . . . "Rings on her fingers . . . Bells on her toes . . . She shall have music wherever she goes . . ."

Katie is growing up without one single memory of her father.

The buzz of the intercom from the lobby meant that Eric Bennett had arrived. "Send him up, please," she directed the doorman.

"Who is it?" Katie asked as she scrambled off the bed.

"A friend of Mommy's. His name is Mr. Bennett."

Eighty-year-old Wilma Potters, who lived in the building, was Katie's favorite babysitter, as active and alert as someone half her age. She and Katie planned to make chocolate-chip cookies and read a book until Katie's bedtime. Wilma had gotten up to answer the door when Lane came into the living room.

"I'll get it, Wilma," Lane said.

The elevator was directly across from the apartment. She heard it whir to a stop but waited until the bell rang before she opened the door.

Her first impression was that Eric Bennett was taller than she had realized. Not much but a little. Fleetingly she remembered that the boots she had been wearing that day had higher heels than she liked. They had been an impulse buy.

At first glance his expression seemed grave, but then his smile was warm. Their greetings of "Hello, Eric," and "Hello, Lane," were said simultaneously as he stepped into the apartment.

Katie had run up to stand by Lane. "I'm Katie Kurner," she announced.

"And I'm Eric Bennett."

"Hello, Eric. It's nice to meet you," Katie began.

"Katie, what did I tell you?" Lane admonished her.

"That I must call big people by their last names. I forgot." She turned and pointed to Wilma Potters. "And this is my babysitter, Mrs. Potters. We're going to bake cookies now."

"Will you save one for me when I bring Mommy home after dinner?"

"I'll save you two," Katie promised.

After a kiss from Katie and an agreement that she would go to bed at eight thirty, they left the apartment. Three minutes later they were on the street and Eric was signaling for a cab. It was five minutes before an empty one came by. "In the old days a car would have been waiting for us," he said as he opened the door for her.

"I can assure you that growing up I was not used to a chauffeur-driven car." But you were, she thought, as Eric gave an address on Fifty-Sixth Street.

"Have you been to Il Tinello?" he asked her.

"Yes, I have," Lane said quietly.

"Then you know that it's quiet and the northern Italian cuisine is delicious."

"Yes I do."

Why that place? Lane wondered. It had been where she and Ken went regularly during their courtship and in the brief year after they married.

"Your Katie is delightful," Eric was saying, "and she's such a pretty little girl."

They were on safe territory. "Well, of course to me she's the most glorious child in the world."

Eric paused. "I understand that Katie's father died before she was born."

68

"Yes he did." Of course Eric Googled me, Lane thought. I Googled everything about him and his family. Especially his daddy dearest.

She knew that Parker Bennett had been born Joseph Bennett but at twenty-one had legally changed his first name to Parker. She knew that he had gone to the City College of New York for two years and from there had received a scholarship to Harvard, then gotten an MBA from Yale. She knew that his rise in a Wall Street brokerage firm had been steady and swift. By the time he married Anne Nelson, a twenty-two-year-old secretary in the firm, he was, at twenty-seven, well on his way up the corporate ladder.

When they reached the restaurant, Mario, the owner, said, "Welcome home," his usual warm greeting to longtime customers. But then, smiling at Lane, he added, "Mrs. Kurner, it has been too long."

"I know it has, Mario," Lane said, "and I'm happy to be here again."

Mario escorted them to a table. When they were seated Eric said, "He called you Mrs. Kurner. I would guess that you used to come here with your husband."

"Yes I did. But that was over five years ago. Harmon is my maiden name. I kept it for business."

The waiter was approaching their table. "Would you like a drink or do you prefer wine?" Eric asked.

"Wine."

"White or red?"

"Red if that's all right with you."

"It's exactly right."

Lane watched as Eric examined the wine list. When he ordered she knew it was one of the most expensive vintages on the list. Her stepfather was a wine connoisseur. When she was in Washington and went out to dinner with him and her mother, he always ordered one of the fine wines.

So much for everything being clawed back, she thought.

As though he could read her mind Eric said, "Considering my situation, I'd like to get something out of the way. I never worked for or with my father. He wanted me to make it on my own, just as he did. Maybe he intentionally kept me away from his firm because he knew how things were going to end. Looking back, if he did steal that money, he didn't want any suggestion that I was involved." He looked directly across the table. "I wasn't," he said. "I hope that you can believe that."

"I wouldn't be here if I thought you were

involved in that situation," Lane said.

Over dinner they talked the way people who are beginning to know each other converse. Lane told him that she had gone to Sacred Heart Academy in Washington from kindergarten through high school and then to NYU. "The minute I started living in New York I knew that this is where I wanted to be," she explained, "but then when I graduated I realized that I didn't want to be a teacher."

"And you went to the Fashion Institute," Eric said.

"You did Google me thoroughly."

"Yes, I did. I hope you don't mind but I wanted to know more about you."

Lane turned the implied compliment away with a laugh. "Fortunately, I have nothing to hide." Realizing the implication of her words, she wanted to bite her tongue.

"And fortunately, despite the general perception, neither do I," Eric replied with a smile. Then he changed the subject. "What's it like working for Glady? When she was working on the Greenwich house, I thought she was the most impossible bully I'd ever met. The poor workmen cringed when she walked into the room."

She is an impossible bully, Lane thought, but I'm not going to admit it to you. "I love working for Glady," she said honestly. "I know what you mean, but believe it or not, she does have the proverbial heart of gold."

"I know she does, at least on some levels. She is redecorating my mother's town house in Montclair without charge."

"See what I mean?"

Over dessert Eric talked about his father. 'It would be impossible to describe a better dad," he said. "Busy as he was, my mother and I were his first priority. He never missed a school event that I was involved in. When I joined the Boy Scouts I got it in my head that I wanted to go camping. He told me he'd go with me. He bought all the gear, learned how to pitch a tent, and found a camping ground in the Adirondacks. We made a fire and cooked over it. Everything we cooked got burned. When we went to bed, we were both cold. We couldn't get to sleep. Finally at about eleven o'clock he said, 'Eric, do you think as I do that this is a ridiculous situation?' When I fervently agreed, he said, 'Then let's bag it. We'll just leave all this paraphernalia here. I'll call the office of this place and tell them it's theirs. They can raffle it off or give it away.' "

"So I guess you never made it to Eagle Scout," Lane said.

"Actually I did. I didn't want to be a quitter."

He took a sip of coffee. "Lane, although I lost a lot of clients because of my father, I'm still a good trader, and I'm rebuilding. But I gave every nickel I had saved or invested to the government to help pay back the people who lost their money."

"Do people know that?"

"No. I requested that it be kept quiet. I knew what the response would be, that I was just trying to look good."

"Damned if you do and damned if you don't," Lane suggested.

"I would say so."

This time they caught a cab immediately after leaving the restaurant. At the apartment building Lane started to say good night but Eric said, "I'll see you to your door."

When they got off the elevator, he asked, "I promise you that I won't delay, but is it possible to see if Katie left me those two cookies?"

"I know she did. Come on in."

The cookies were on a paper plate on the coffee table. Katie had drawn a smiley face on the plate.

Eric reached down, picked up one of them, and took a bite out of it. "Delicious," he pronounced. "Thank Katie for me. Tell her I love it with lots of chocolate chips, just the way she made them." He picked up the plate and said, "I'll eat this one on my way down in the elevator. Lane, I've enjoyed this evening very much. And now, as promised, I'm out of here."

Less than a minute later Lane heard the whine of the elevator going down. Then Wilma Potters came down the hall. After Katie was in bed Wilma had made it a habit to sit on the comfortable chair in the small den at the end of the hall and watch television.

"Katie went to bed promptly at eight thirty," she volunteered. "Did you have a nice time?"

Lane hesitated, then answered, "I had a very nice time, Mrs. Potters. I really did."

12

Marge O'Brian sat nervously in the anteroom waiting to be called into Rudy Schell's office. What did I do wrong? she asked herself. Why would the FBI want to talk to me? It had been only yesterday that she had gone to New Jersey following the moving van that had brought the contents that had been selected from the Bennett mansion for Anne Bennett's new home in Montclair, New Jersey.

With the help of Lane Harmon and two workmen Lane brought with her, she had unpacked boxes of china and books and clothing so that when Mrs. Bennett arrived the next day the town house would not be cluttered. Lane had told her that the spread and drapes and vanity skirt would be in next week and she would be there to see that everything was exactly right.

She's such a nice person, Marge thought, and the town house is so pretty. The furniture fit in like it was made for those rooms. And it's so cozy. When Mr. Bennett was around he filled the mansion with his presence. But poor Mrs. Bennett rattling around there alone was kind of pathetic.

Why did the FBI call her again last night? She already talked to them two years ago. What did they mean when they said they just wanted to ask her a few questions? They didn't think she was in on the money disappearing, did they? No, of course not. All they have to do is take a look at my bank account, she thought.

I'm going to miss Mrs. Bennett and Eric, she thought. They were always so nice to me. Mr. Bennett was too, she added defensively, but I was kind of scared of him. When he got mad, *wow!* His rages came on suddenly. Like the morning his new Bentley had a stain on the cushion of the front seat because the chauffeur had spilled coffee when he was waiting for him in front of the house. He had fired the chauffeur on the spot but then came into the house and started shouting at Roger, the butler, who had found him.

"The next time I hire one of your slob friends and have a problem it's your neck too," he had said.

When Mrs. Bennett said, "Parker, all

Roger did was call the agency and they recommended the driver," he had turned on her too. "Anne, can you ever get over treating the help as your dear friends?" he had snapped. "It's too bad you never could understand that you're not helping out in your father's delicatessen anymore."

But that was only one part of him. The next day he rehired the chauffeur, apologized to the butler, and bought Mrs. Bennett a gorgeous diamond pin. I saw the note he had put on it. It read, "To my long-suffering darling."

"Mrs. O'Brian, Mr. Schell will see you now."

With lagging steps Marge followed the man into Rudy Schell's austere office. But the moment she walked in the door it was a relief when the man behind the desk stood up and with a welcoming smile greeted her and invited her to sit down. He can't be going to arrest me or something, she thought.

She quickly found out that that was the last thing on Agent Schell's mind. "Mrs. O'Brian, it's been almost two years since you spoke to one of our agents. Now that Mrs. Bennett is moving to New Jersey, are you planning to continue to work for her?"

"I'm sorry to say that I'm not," Marge said. "I always went home at night. There's no way I can make the trip from Connecticut to New Jersey five days a week, and even if she wanted me to live in, there's no way I'd want to be that far from my grandkids. They're always over at my house."

Rudy Schell nodded. "I can understand that. Please don't think I'm asking you to be disloyal, but as you must know Parker Bennett has ruined many lives. People who trusted in him have lost their homes, their retirement funds, and their ability to help their families. But I am asking you to think. Was there ever a time when you overheard either Mrs. Bennett or her son indicate that they knew whether or not Parker Bennett is alive?"

Marge sat quietly. There was one time. Only two weeks ago. It was the night Mrs. Bennett shouted at Eric. But it wouldn't be fair to repeat that. Unless it was just the stress of her life causing it, Mrs. Bennett was slipping into early dementia. She repeated herself a lot. Anyhow, what she said sounded crazy.

"Mrs. O'Brian" — Rudy Schell's voice was encouraging — "just looking at your expression, I have a feeling that you are trying to decide whether or not to tell me something. Please remember that if Eric Bennett and his mother are innocent of any knowledge of Parker Bennett's crime, we stand ready to publicly clear their names. As it is there is plenty of suspicion that both of them were in on it. But if you heard anything that might help us to recover that money you really must share it with us."

Hesitantly Marge began, "Less than a week ago after dinner I couldn't help but hear Mrs. Bennett scream at Eric."

Rudy Schell did not let a flicker of emotion show in his eyes or manner. "What was she saying when she screamed at him?"

"I can't give you her exact words but it was something like this: 'Eric, I know your father is alive and you know it too. Tell him to call me. Tell him I don't care what he's done. Tell him to call me.' "

Marge took a long breath. "But remember, I think Mrs. Bennett may be going into dementia and maybe that's something she just got into her head."

"It may have been," Schell said soothingly, "but it was right for you to share it with me. Now I must ask that if you speak to either of the Bennetts you will not tell them that we have had this meeting."

When the door closed behind Marge O'Brian's departing figure, Rudy leaned back in his chair. I always thought that guy was involved, he thought. Even his mother

thinks he is.
  Now, how do we prove it?

13

Anne Bennett slept late the first night she stayed in her new home. When she woke her head felt clearer than it had in months. Or maybe even since that terrible day that Parker had disappeared from the sailboat.

He had gone for the weekend to St. John, where he kept his sailboat. Eric was supposed to fly down with him on the plane but was delayed at his office and didn't arrive until the next day.

I begged Parker to wait until Eric could sail with him but he got angry, Anne thought. He asked me if I thought he was incompetent. I knew enough not to say another word. He went out that morning alone. The sea was choppy. He never came back. They found the sailboat smashed against the rocks in Tortola.

She blinked back tears, which so often spilled over when she thought of Parker. It was nine o'clock and time to get up. She threw back the comforter, reached for her robe, eased her feet into her slippers, and went downstairs to the kitchen. She turned on the Keurig coffeemaker and waited until the "ready to brew" indicator went on. Less than a minute later she was carrying the cup to the table. I don't feel like eating anything now, she thought.

Then she glanced out the side window that looked over the driveway. Sitting at his kitchen table was that nice man, Tony Russo, who had come over and introduced himself when Eric drove her here yesterday a few minutes after the moving van arrived.

He had said that he had just moved in as well and that he was opening a restaurant on Valley Road. Then he said that he wouldn't delay us but he wanted me to know that he'd be back and forth every day and that I should please call on him if I ever needed assistance of any kind.

Lane had told her that there was a privacy shade being made and would be installed next week when the spread and draperies arrived.

Russo had his computer on the kitchen table. Anne quickly changed seats to avoid catching his eye. I won't have to pull the shade down if I sit in this seat, she thought. I'll just pull it down at night.

She finished the coffee and brewed another cup. While she was waiting she thought again about what she had screamed at Eric last week, that she knew Parker was alive and so did he.

I had too much wine at dinner, she reminded herself again. The idea that Parker was still alive was probably wishful thinking. She still could feel the thrill of the moment all those years ago when Parker had called her from his office and asked her to have dinner with him. She was so scared that it had been obvious from that day on the subway steps that she had a terrible crush on him.

He was so handsome and so smart. It got around the office that he had received a huge year-end bonus. That night after work I went straight to the delicatessen to tell Mom and Daddy that I was going out with him.

Mom was delighted. Daddy was dismissive. "Why wouldn't he ask you out? You must be the prettiest girl in that company. If he acts like one of those playboy big shots and tries to make a pass at you, you've got to promise me that you'll march out of that restaurant and take a cab home."

Daddy got even more upset when he

heard that Parker was picking me up in a car.

"You could have met him at the restaurant and taken a cab home."

By the time Parker and I were married six months later Daddy still didn't trust him, she mused. He didn't like it that Parker insisted we get married at that ritzy St. Ignatius Loyola Church in Manhattan. Parker said that he didn't want his friends trekking out to our parish church in Brooklyn. It was a big wedding and the reception was at The Plaza. Daddy was angry that Parker insisted on paying for everything, even my wedding dress. Parker said that he didn't want me to buy something off the rack in Macy's.

Daddy was never impressed by him . . . He said, "Anne, what scares me is that I feel it in my veins that that guy is a phony. He may make a lot of money but only a phony would change a good name like Joseph to one that he thinks is high-class."

Anne smiled. When Dad wanted to get Parker's goat, he called him Joey.

We were so happy together all those years. Every morning when he left for the office he would always tell me how much he would miss me all day. And I would say that I'd miss him too. It was our little joke. Even that last day when he was getting on the plane to St. John he said to me, "I'll always miss you so much."

Parker wasn't religious. What did he mean when he said, "I'll always miss you so much"? Even though he went to church with me now and then, he certainly didn't believe in the hereafter. He believed that when we die, it's all over. Then what did he mean?

And why did I scream at poor Eric that he knew his father was alive? Was it only because I had had too much wine that night?

Anne finished her second cup of coffee and pushed back the terrible and unwelcome thought that she might have inherited her father's intuition.

14

On Monday morning Eric Bennett entered the office of Patrick Adams, founder of the security firm that bore his name.

A former New York State senator, Adams, during his ten-year tenure, had been outraged by the constant evidence of graft he witnessed at sessions of the Albany legislature. Deciding to retire and do something about it, he had opened the security agency. Within two years he had earned the reputation of successfully unearthing fraud, not only in government-related crimes but also insider trading.

He was astonished to learn that Eric Bennett, son of the notorious swindler Parker Bennett, had made an appointment to see him.

Like the vast majority of the public, he believed that Eric had worked hand in glove with his father to steal the money from the Bennett Fund.

Fifty-two years old, wide-bodied but in shape, with a full head of mostly gray hair and an aura of confidence about himself, Adams was a formidable man.

The fact that Bennett arrived precisely at ten impressed him favorably. He had no use for people who were chronically late. But he was equally dismissive of people who arrived much too early. It was a sign of insecurity, which made him suspicious.

His secretary escorted Eric Bennett in. Adams's first impression of him was favorable. Bennett was dressed in a well-cut gray suit. The sleeves of his shirt had cuffs. The cuff links were unobtrusive, small black stones. His polite reserve as he greeted Adams was a surprise. Adams had expected him to appear nervous.

Invited to be seated, Bennett took the chair directly in front of Adams's desk.

"I'll get right to the point," he said calmly. "Unless you are blind, deaf, and dumb, which I certainly know you're not, I don't have to explain anything about my father, Parker Bennett, and what he is accused of doing."

"Accused," Adams thought. How about, I know what your father did?

His answer to Bennett was given in the same direct tone. "Yes, I am aware of the circumstances surrounding your father."

"Well then, you are also aware of the circumstances surrounding me," Eric said quietly. "The belief that I was involved in the theft is almost universal. Don't you agree?"

"Yes, I do."

"Then you must understand where I'm coming from. I am absolutely innocent of any involvement in the theft. My computer has been pulled apart. Every investigative agency known to man has worked me over. None of them has been able to tie me to the fraud.

"I love my father dearly. He was a wonderful husband to my mother and a wonderful father to me. I can only conclude that in some way he was mentally ill when he committed these crimes."

"That means he may have been mentally ill when he started the Bennett Fund fifteen years ago," Adams reminded him. "It's obvious that from the beginning it was a well-planned pyramid scheme."

"I am aware of that," Eric said, a trace of defensiveness in his tone. "But the FBI has had no success in finding any evidence that my father is alive or where that money disappeared to. Now I want to retain your firm to investigate the case."

"Do you realize that if we do an investigation it could possibly result in your father spending the rest of his life in prison?"

"I do," Eric said as his eyes moistened and his voice wavered. Then, composing himself, he continued. "If my father is alive, he must be found, and of course the money he stole must be returned to the investors he cheated."

"Or what's left of it," Adams said dryly. "I warn you that if we do agree to take on this case it will be very expensive."

"I know that. I am a successful trader and the market has been good. In the two years since my father's disappearance I have lived very frugally. I will continue to do so, but I can put down a retainer of fifty thousand dollars. By the time you use that up, I should be able to give you more. If I can't continue to pay you, you can suspend your investigation until I can accumulate more money."

Adams felt a twinge of sympathy for the man sitting opposite him. But the practical side of his nature overrode that feeling immediately.

"What if we take on the investigation and find that you are involved?"

"Then I would expect you to turn me in to the federal prosecutor," Eric said promptly. "But I won't lose any sleep over that possibility."

Adams wondered if he knew what he was getting into as he reached his hand across the desk and said, "We'll take the case, Mr. Bennett. And we will use every resource possible to find your father alive or prove his death, and to locate the missing money."

As he spoke Adams realized that he was thoroughly intrigued by the idea of being paid to search for the missing Parker Bennett.

As for Eric Bennett, he decided there were two possibilities: that he was totally innocent, as he claimed, and wanted to change the public perception of him, or that he was guilty, and also arrogant enough to think that he and his father had planned so carefully that they were beyond the reach of the law.

Adams realized that insider trading cases had begun to seem mundane.

The search for Parker Bennett will be infinitely more challenging, he thought with satisfaction.

15

He had known that they were closing in on him. He was so frantic to get away that he moved most of the money from one Swiss account to the other. He had taped the new account number on the inside of the music box he had given Anne years ago. But when he successfully made his escape, he realized that incredibly, the number he had jotted down was not the new one but the *old* one.

Now he was living comfortably on St. Thomas in a small villa on the Caribbean. He had a new sailboat, not nearly as large or expensive as the one he had set adrift. But it was perfectly satisfactory. He was successfully established in the identity he had long ago created for himself for when the time came to escape. But the money in the old account would soon run out. Water, water everywhere, but not a drop to drink, he thought bitterly.

In St. Thomas he was known as George

Hawkins, a retired engineer who had moved here from England fifteen years ago.

The brown wig he always wore changed his appearance. So did the dark glasses and the putty he expertly applied to change the shape of his nose.

His British passport assured him that if he ever needed to he could relocate, and do it immediately.

The disposable cell phone in his pocket rang. Almost afraid to answer, he picked it up.

"Parker, dear," a woman's voice said, her tone matter-of-fact, "I'm afraid I will need more money soon."

"But I sent an extra million dollars to your account three months ago," he protested. As always, his anger was replaced by fear.

"That was three months ago. I'm redecorating the apartment and I will need more immediately. I'll give you the exact amount when I get it from the decorator."

She had been blackmailing him for two years. There was no way he could refuse her.

"I will wire you the money," he said coldly.

"I knew you would, and I want you to know my lips are sealed. Bye, sweetheart, I miss you."

He did not reply. Instead he broke the connection and for a long time sat at his desk looking at the Caribbean.

It was a beautiful, sun-filled day. The ocean was blue-green. Faint ripples tossed a spray of reflective color on the beach outside his villa. He loved it here. Over the years he had firmly established his identity. On his frequent trips, when he was supposed to be sailing, he came here. He had rigorously cultivated a British accent and it was now second nature. The friends he had carefully chosen years ago completely accepted him for what they thought he was, a rather shy man, a widower who loved sailing. He had told them he was an engineer from England. It was a smooth transition when he came here two years ago and announced that he was retired now and would live on St. Thomas permanently.

He had also taken up golf, and was surprisingly good at it. He only went to public courses. The confines of a private club might have invited intimacy with other members. Familiarity breeds contempt, and in my case possible suspicion, he thought. There was one man he had hooked up with on a foursome on a public course, a self-proclaimed Anglophile, who wanted to discuss with him the many engineers he knew in the London area. He had not gone back to that course again.

She knew he was here. She thought he had access to all the money. She would bleed him forever. She liked to drink. He had seen her get blotto. Not often, but the tendency was there. It was absolutely possible that while drunk she might inadvertently give him away.

He could not let the situation go on. As long as he still lived here, he was in danger from her. He had never thought that he would contemplate the taking of another person's life, but desperate times require desperate measures, he reminded himself coldly.

It was a terrible risk, but he had to go back, get the number from the music box and, to be absolutely sure he was safe, he would put his backup plan into action and move to Switzerland.

He hadn't planned to go sailing today, but when anything troubled him, it became a necessity to be on the boat and feel himself one with the sea and the sky. After all, he had earned that pleasure.

16

Eleanor Becker had been Parker Bennett's secretary for all thirteen years the Bennett investment firm had existed.

Then fifty years old, childless, she had been approached by Parker at the brokerage firm where they both worked. He had told her he was going to form his own company and wanted her to go with him.

It had been an easy decision for her to make. Parker was a charismatic man, and always so courteous to her. The broker she was working for had been volatile; he was perfectly pleasant in the morning, but when the closing bell rang at four thirty, he was a different person if his trading had been on a downward spiral.

Jekyll and Hyde, she used to think when he came charging to her desk. "Did you do this yet? Why not? Did you follow up on that one? Can't you do *anything* right?"

She used to be tempted to ask him why

he didn't save his ill temper for his wife. But of course, that would never have happened. His second wife, twenty-five years younger, wouldn't have taken it.

And so it had been with unmitigated pleasure that she tendered her resignation and went to work for Parker. The salary was much better. The Christmas bonus refurnished the living room of their modest home in Yonkers. When her husband, Frank, became ill with diabetes, Parker had made her promise that any bills not covered by her insurance be sent to him.

I never was involved with the firm's finances, believe it or not, she thought defensively. The two years Parker Bennett had been missing had been a constant nightmare. She knew the FBI believed that she was involved in the scheme. They had questioned her for hours on end. And last week she had testified for several hours before the grand jury. She had been informed by the federal prosecutor that she was a target of the grand jury investigation. The prosecutor had invited her to testify if she wished. She had spent hours with her attorney, Grover Johnson, going over the pros and cons of appearing. He had warned her that he would not be permitted to be with her inside the grand jury room as she was being questioned. He was also very concerned that anything she said could be used against her later on if she was indicted.

Eleanor had asked Grover what her chances were of not being indicted if she didn't appear. He had been candid that she would almost certainly be indicted. "Then Grover, I really have nothing to lose. I'm going to tell the truth and maybe they will realize that I am innocent. I am going to testify."

The prosecutor had quizzed her relentlessly. In her mind she reviewed his questions and her answers.

"Mrs. Becker, isn't it a fact that you helped to convince people to invest in the Parker Bennett Fund?"

"It's not that I convinced them, it's that Mr. Bennett would have me send out letters inviting people to come in for a visit and learn about the fund."

"How did he select the names of those people?"

"Part of my job was to read a lot of newspapers and create a list of people with small businesses, or people who might have had some recognition from their community."

"Exactly what kind of recognition?"

"Well, the story might be about a small business celebrating its fiftieth anniversary.

I'd get the person's name and background for Mr. Bennett."

"How many of these would you give to him a day?"

"Some days as little as five, or as many as twenty."

"What came next?"

"I had a form letter ready to send."

"What kind of form letter?"

"Congratulating the person on whatever the reasons for choosing him or her, and inviting him or her to come to the office and have a cup of tea or coffee with Mr. Bennett."

"How about lottery winners? Did he write to them?"

"If they won only a few million dollars, he did. The big winners he stayed away from. He said every big money manager would be after them, 'like flies to honey.' He said that he was only interested in making money for the small investor."

"When the small investor came to the office, what happened?"

"As you probably know, Mr. Bennett had a very large office. There was a grouping of a couch and comfortable chairs around a wide coffee table. I would bring in coffee and crumb cake or doughnuts before lunch, and tea and little sandwiches in the afternoon."

"Then what happened?"

"Mr. Bennett would sit down with the people and chat with them. Then he would ask me to bring out some account statements of people who were current investors. Of course he had me black out their names."

"But it showed that their accounts were making money?"

"Yes."

"Was there a minimum that could be invested?"

"Ten thousand dollars."

"What were the new investors told when they began investing in the Parker Bennett Fund?"

"If, for example, after one year their ten-thousand-dollar investment had not gone up ten percent, the investor could take it out and Mr. Bennett would give them their investment back and a thousand dollars, the ten-percent return the fund had averaged. But if investors took their money out, they were never again allowed to invest in the Parker Fund."

"Did people often take their money out of the fund?"

"No, hardly ever. They were getting monthly statements showing them how much their money had grown. They stayed in because they wanted their money to keep growing."

"Did those investors who left get their promised ten-percent return?"

"Yes."

"Those investors who stayed in the fund, did they tend to put more of their savings in?"

"Yes."

"And what was the average return on their investment?"

"Ten percent."

"After a few years did Parker Bennett start to take on wealthy clients?"

"Oh yes, he did. People came to him on their own."

"When that happened, did you continue to send out letters inviting small investors in?"

"Yes, but not as many as I did in the early days."

"Why was that?"

"Because we didn't have to. The investors we had were very happy and they were recommending the Parker Fund to their friends, relatives, and coworkers. We were growing so fast I didn't have time to search for new investors."

"You have worked for brokerage firms

since you were twenty-one years old. Didn't you find those returns suspiciously high?"

"I had witnessed what a genius Parker Bennett was in the other firm. I believed in him and trusted him."

"Didn't you think that your salary and bonus were unusually high?"

"I thought he was very generous."

"What did you think when he continued paying for your husband's medical bills?"

"I was overwhelmed."

"And when your husband was forced to retire because of his illness, what did you think when Bennett paid off the mortgage on your house?"

"I broke down and cried."

She knew that the prosecutors were going to indict her. "My husband and I had to take out a new mortgage to keep paying our medical bills," she had burst out.

When she was finally finished, she left the room in tears. Grover Johnson, who had anxiously waited outside, embraced her and tried to calm her down as she sobbed, "I don't think they believed me."

That was another thing. She and Frank had been horrified at how much it cost to hire a lawyer and how much their ongoing case had been running them. Frank exclaimed, "Whoever said, 'There are no

101

lawyers in heaven' was right."

They were supposed to hear from Johnson this afternoon. Nervously the two of them sat in the kitchen having a cup of tea. Frank was thinner now, but still had those wrinkles around his eyes and lips that showed how easily he smiled.

He was not smiling now, and certainly she wasn't. Her hand was trembling as she lifted the cup to her lips. The strain was so unbearable that her eyes were always watering. And a sudden sound could make her gasp in fear. Her cell phone rang. The ID showed that it was Grover Johnson. "If it's Johnson, make it short," Frank warned. "The minute he dials, the clock starts ticking."

"Mrs. Becker?"

He sounds worried, Eleanor thought. Her grip on the phone tightened.

"Yes."

"Mrs. Becker, I am so sorry to tell you that the grand jury has voted to indict you as a co-conspirator of Parker Bennett."

17

The weekend was cold but beautiful. Lane took Katie ice-skating in Rockefeller Plaza. She skated well enough, but Katie was a natural. She had started skating the year before and nothing made Katie happier than to be at the rink. Eric Bennett had sent Katie a note thanking her for the cookies and asking if she also made oatmeal cookies with raisins. Those were his other favorite. He had closed by writing, "I hope to see you soon, Katie. Your friend, Eric Bennett."

He had not phoned Lane. She wondered if the note to Katie was simply a charming gesture or if he meant it when he said he would see her soon. It was disturbing to her how pleased she would be if he asked her to have dinner with him again. She had had dates with a number of men in these past few years and enjoyed them. But emotionally she had never felt the spark she experienced when she was with Eric

Bennett. On Sunday evening she and Katie went to a movie and had dinner at McDonald's, Katie's favorite restaurant. On Monday, Glady informed her that she had done a number of preliminary sketches and chosen colors to show to "Sally," as she referred to the Countess de la Marco. "It's at nine thirty tomorrow morning," she informed Lane, "so be sure to be on time."

"I'm always in before nine, Glady," Lane said, amused, "and you know it. Or if you want, I could meet you at her apartment?" She knew that that would bring a definite no. Glady liked the image of herself being followed by an assistant who was carrying sketches, swatches, and books of antique furniture and carpets.

"We'll meet in the lobby," Glady said crisply.

At nine fifteen the next morning Lane made sure she was in the Fifth Avenue lobby only to find Glady already there. They waited until twenty-seven minutes past nine, when Glady asked the desk clerk to call the apartment of the Countess de la Marco and announce that Ms. Harper was here. Nothing about me, as usual, Lane thought. I might as well be invisible! It was a typical Glady performance.

A male voice at the other end said, "Send her up, please." The butler was waiting for them when they came out of the private elevator.

"The countess will receive you in the library," he said, and led them down the hallway to the left.

"Receive us," Glady muttered as Lane tried to hide a smile.

Countess Sylvie de la Marco was sitting on a red velvet couch. A pot of coffee and three cups were set on the long glass-top table in front of her. She did not get up to greet them, but her smile was pleasant enough.

"How nice of you," Glady said sincerely as the butler poured the coffee. But after having a few sips she got down to business.

"We will not be making any serious architectural changes," she announced as she took the bag Lane had been carrying. "I estimate that the redecoration, including a few antiques and artwork, will come in at about five million dollars. I have preliminary sketches of the rooms on this floor and how we will deal with them to create diversity, harmony, and understated elegance."

The countess went over the sketches, carefully examining them one by one.

Then Glady got up. "I suggest that we go

over the sketches as we walk through the rooms. But first you need to take care of the contract and provide the two million dollars that is required on signing."

Lane observed that the countess did not even bat a false eyelash. "That will be fine," Sylvie said. "I'll meet you in the drawing room. But first I have an important phone call to make."

As they walked down the hallway Glady snapped, "What did you think when she referred to the living room as the drawing room?" Not waiting for Lane to answer, she said, "You can bet your life that she learned that expression when she read some trashy nineteenth-century romance novel."

For a long moment they stood at the door of the largest room of the apartment. "All that glitters is not gold," Glady murmured to Lane with ill-concealed contempt. She studied the ornate yellow brocade draperies with heavy gold-colored tassels.

"Oh, come on, Glady," Lane protested. "She knows this place is tawdry, but that's why she's paying you a lot of money to redo it. Just think how pleasant she has been to us this morning."

As always, when she was crossed, Glady's eyebrows shot up. "Lane, you must learn not to be so willing to think everyone you meet could be your new best friend. The countess has told anyone who will listen that this place was decorated in such garish taste because her predecessor, the second Countess de la Marco, had commissioned it that way. The fact is that everyone knows who called the shots every step of the way. This was Sally Chico's idea of high class and there were lots of jokes about it in the society columns. She throws a lot of parties, and she read that it was called "Sylvie's golden cage."

Behind Glady, Lane could see that the countess was approaching them from down the hallway.

"What colors would you suggest for this room?" Lane asked Glady, her tone a little louder than necessary.

For an instant Glady looked startled. Then she realized that Lane was cautioning her to stop disparaging her new client. Without missing a beat she said, "This room will be very beautiful, a suitable background for the countess."

It was immediately obvious that de la Marco had overheard and picked up the sarcasm in Glady's tone. Her eyes narrowed and her voice lost the friendly tone she had been exhibiting on this second visit.

"For your fee, Ms. Harper, I would expect

that you would be able to achieve a suitable background for me."

Glady had better be careful, Lane thought. But she's right. Underneath that pleasant demeanor, this is one tough lady.

Of course, Glady was not intimidated. "Countess, if you feel the cost of this renovation is beyond your means, I would be happy to withdraw and terminate our contract."

"That will not be necessary," the countess snapped, turned on her heel, and walked away.

When the countess was safely out of earshot, Glady said, "Did you notice that she never even blinked when I gave her the estimate for this job? It's obvious she has a boyfriend."

"I looked her up," Lane said. "She tried to break her prenup, but got nowhere."

"I know that. The amount she got was sealed. But people say the family managed to put a lot of the count's money in a trust, because of his obvious dementia. Sally didn't get that much comparatively, not enough for the way she is throwing money around now. You saw that the minute I gave her the final estimate she said that she had to make a phone call. She has to have a new 'big bucks' boyfriend. My guess is that it's

108

one of those Russian billionaires."

Without stopping for breath Glady added, "Of course, she was Parker Bennett's girlfriend for years. She may have been building a golden nest egg before he disappeared."

18

Jonathan Pierce, alias Tony Russo, watched, amused, as a van marked "H&L Security" pulled up to the curb opposite Anne Bennett's town house. The security system had already been installed. He knew that the purpose of this service was to be sure Bennett's new home was not bugged.

He had seen Eric Bennett enter the town house a few hours earlier. That was unusual. In the ten days she had been here Eric had established a pattern of having dinner with his mother every other night. At least you have to give him credit for being a thoughtful son, Jon thought. But if he's innocent, why would he be so worried about bugs in the town house? Is he afraid his mother will let something slip about his father's whereabouts, or the missing money?

In the past week he had managed to establish a tentative friendship with Anne Bennett without being too obvious about it.

The mail was usually delivered around nine o'clock. He would watch for the truck to arrive, and when he was on his way out to retrieve his mail the door to Anne Bennett's town house would open. It seemed to him that she was on the lookout for the mailman. Was it because she expected a communication from her husband?

He was trying to establish her pattern of behavior. On Sunday morning she had gone out at quarter of ten. He had followed her to the Church of the Immaculate Conception, where she had attended Mass. A few days later she had also gone to a local hairdresser. He knew that her fancy New York salon had told her not to come back; after that she had had a hairdresser come to the house in Connecticut.

Maybe she had counted on making a fresh start here in New Jersey? He even hoped that this was true, but only if she was not involved in the disappearance of all that money.

Surreptitiously Jon glanced to his left. He was sitting at the breakfast room table, which he had turned into his desk. Anne Bennett left her shade up during the day. He knew that most of the time she sat in a chair that did not place her facing him. But sometimes she either forgot or didn't care.

111

Her son never arrived before six P.M. The only other person who had been there twice that week was the interior decorator, Lane Harmon.

Jon had checked her out too. Lane was the daughter of the late congressman and her stepfather was a very powerful columnist. It would be very foolish of her to get involved with the Bennett family. Maybe even dangerous. It wouldn't do her any good if Anne Bennett unintentionally let anything slip to her about where her husband was hiding.

His phone rang. It was Rudy Schell. "Anything up, Jon?"

"I just saw a guy pretending to be from an alarm service going into the Bennett town house. I'm sure he was there to sweep for bugs. I'll get into the town house Sunday morning when Anne Bennett goes to church again."

"How often is the son there?"

"Every other night for dinner, as far as I can see."

"Who cooks?" was the next question.

"There's an upscale restaurant that delivers whenever Eric comes to New Jersey. "The other nights she seems to make do with leftovers."

"How about a housekeeper?"

112

"Nothing so far. But there's a cleaning service that works in a lot of the places here. They rang her doorbell the other day. I wouldn't be surprised if she hires them. My guess is that she might not want a daily housekeeper."

"That's too bad. It might be interesting to hear what she might let slip to a daily housekeeper." Rudy Schell ended the conversation in his usual brisk way. "Keep me posted."

19

It was with dismay that Sean Cunningham learned from the TV morning news that Eleanor Becker had been indicted as a co-conspirator of Parker Bennett. In the past two years he had made it his business to visit Eleanor a number of times. Knowing her, he absolutely believed that the only crime she had committed was to trust Parker Bennett so blindly. The indictment meant that she would be arraigned before a judge, have to post bail, and then have the continuing expense of a defense lawyer. Her trial might be as long as two years away. In that time the worry and the expense could break her down, physically and psychologically.

In the course of his career Sean had dealt with patients with that kind of problem. If by some miracle Eleanor was acquitted, it would be too late to undo the damage that had been done. She would be emotionally exhausted and financially strapped.

He decided to call her and ask if he could pay her a visit tomorrow afternoon.

Today he already had an appointment with Ranger Cole. He had been calling Ranger every day since the funeral service. Ranger had neither answered the calls nor responded to the messages he left. Then Ranger had finally called him back yesterday afternoon. He said, "I'm sorry, doctor, it's real nice of you to worry about me. I should've called you sooner." His voice had been monotone and lifeless.

"I'm concerned about you, Ranger," Sean told him frankly. "I know what it's like to lose your wife. Mine died five years ago. The first year is the worst. But trust me, it does get better. How about I stop by your place tomorrow? Maybe around three o'clock."

"Yeah, sure, if you want."

Now Sean looked at his watch. It was nine thirty. That meant he had five hours to work on the book he was writing. The title was *Responding to Stress.*

Without using anyone's real name, he had just started on the book when the Parker Bennett Investment Fund was revealed to be a fraud. Because of that he had more than enough cases for the section about sudden financial change. Another section would deal with reacting to the death of a loved one. I'm in both of those categories, Sean thought as he looked at the framed picture on his desk. It had been taken when he and Nona were in Monaco. They were walking outside the palace there. A photographer who was nearby had snapped the picture and sold it to them.

It had been one of those perfect days, Sean mused. The sun was shining. It was about seventy degrees. We were hand in hand in the picture and we both were smiling. To him the picture was a reflection of their life together. I miss Nona so terribly, he thought, and there are times that I have to remind myself I should be grateful for those forty-five good years.

Restless, he got up and walked across the room. His apartment was in lower Manhattan. From his window he had a clear view of the Statue of Liberty, a sight that never failed to lift his spirits. He knew that he was deeply troubled today, and with good reason. In the last two years Ranger Cole and Eleanor Becker had become his friends. And both had a rocky road ahead.

Sean stretched and returned to his desk. At one o'clock he went into the kitchen and heated the beef vegetable soup his housekeeper had prepared for his lunch. He

116

brought it back to his desk and as he sipped it, he acknowledged that the writing was not going well. He could not concentrate on the cases he had selected to write about today. He felt every one of his seventy years. It was a relief at two thirty to put his pen down, go to the closet, and get out his coat, scarf, and gloves. Five minutes later, his steps brisk, he was walking to the subway. It was two express stops to Forty-Second Street, where Ranger lived in a converted tenement on Eighth Avenue.

Ranger Cole regretted the fact that he'd agreed to see Dr. Cunningham. He didn't need to hear again that the doctor's wife was dead and how well he was doing. Ranger knew that he would never feel better. He had taken a spoonful of Judy's ashes and put them in a small medicine vial. It was the one where Judy had kept her pain pills. He had tied the vial with a cord and hung it around his neck. It made him feel close to her. That was what he needed.

The doorbell rang. I'm not going to answer it, he thought. But Cunningham was persistent. He kept pushing and pushing the bell. Then he shouted, "Ranger, I know you're in there. Open the door. We need to talk."

Ranger wrapped his hand around the vial. "Leave me alone," he shouted. "Go away! I want to be alone with Judy."

20

"The accessories for Anne Bennett's bedroom will be installed on Wednesday," was Glady's greeting to Lane on Monday morning. "You'd better go over there and make sure they did everything the way I ordered."

Her voice was peevish, but Lane thought she knew why.

They weren't getting paid for this job. Even though Glady planned to tack the expense onto the countess's bill, Lane would need to be there to supervise the installation of the window hangings and be sure that no mistake had been made in the execution of the color scheme. Glady had turned over the details of jobs for more of their smaller clients to Lane to follow through on. Now she was impatient because Lane would be wasting time at Anne Bennett's home.

Lane had mixed feelings about going

there. She liked Anne Bennett and would enjoy seeing her. On the other hand, Eric Bennett had not called her again. Almost certainly he would not be at his mother's home on a weekday morning, but even so, the possibility was disturbing.

It would be awkward to run into him. That's the problem with any kind of business-related friendships, she thought. Better to stay away from them.

"Shall I repeat what you obviously didn't hear me say?" Glady asked sarcastically.

Startled, Lane said, "Oh, Glady. I'm sorry."

"What I said to you was they'll be there at eleven to install everything. When they're finished, don't let Anne Bennett persuade you to stay for lunch."

I'll balk if she tells me to go to a McDonald's drive-through, Lane thought.

Every once in a while it was obvious that Glady realized she had gone too far.

"What I mean is, have lunch somewhere after you leave her. All you'll hear from her will be her breast-beating about her innocent husband."

Then her expression became serious. "Lane, we know the countess did not get that much after the count died. If she has a billionaire boyfriend, no one knows who he is.

"And that leaves her sugar daddy, Parker Bennett," Glady snarled. "If he's alive and she's bleeding him for money, my guess is he could be ruthless. And don't forget he has a son who might be ruthless about preserving the stolen money too."

That night Lane did not sleep well. As usual she went to bed at ten o'clock, fell asleep, then awakened at midnight, her eyes wide open, her body taut.

At three A.M., still awake, she was startled to see the door of her room pushed open.

It was Katie. "I had a bad dream," she said quietly as she climbed into bed and snuggled against Lane.

"Tell me about it."

"It was that I was looking for you and you weren't anywhere I looked. I was scared."

"Oh, sweetie, no matter where you are, I promise you I'll be there too."

But even as she made the promise and felt Katie's body relax, she remembered that as a child she had had a similar dream.

She had been running through the house looking for her father. That was after he died in the plane crash in California.

If something happened to me, there was no one who could give Katie the emotional

121

support she would need.

Her mother, of course, would welcome Katie. But Lane knew that her stepfather, Dwight, would resent the intrusion of a young child into his home.

So the answer is that nothing had better happen to me for the next twenty or so years, Lane decided.

And, dear God, don't let anything happen to Katie.

Her grip tightened around her child as she drifted off to sleep.

21

On Tuesday morning Parker Bennett poured himself a second cup of coffee as he reviewed his plan.

Nothing should be done in haste. That was how he had jotted down the wrong account number when he was getting out of the country.

With all the years he had managed to pull the wool over everyone's eyes, he had made that terrible mistake because he was panicking at the imminence of discovery. He could not make any mistake again.

He would tell his friends in St. Thomas that he had been called back to England for a special project for the government. He had signed a confidentiality agreement and could not discuss details with them.

He would arrange for the housekeeper to come in every other week so that there would be no hint that he was going away permanently. He would arrange for the bank to pay her and the utilities and the taxes on a monthly basis.

He would leave the sailboat tied to his dock and covered.

On his laptop, he researched real estate for sale in Switzerland.

One villa caught his eye. It was near Geneva, which meant that he would have access to both the airport and the railroad station.

He had no intention of staying in Switzerland during the entire winter. But once he had established a presence there, he could certainly take frequent vacations in France. How he would miss his sailboat. Never mind, he told himself. You can always get one on the Riviera.

Of course there is always the danger of running into one of his Wall Street friends. But so far his disguise had held despite the fact that his picture ran in the newspapers and magazines with some frequency.

He went to the front door and retrieved the *Wall Street Journal,* the *New York Times,* the *New York Post,* and the *Virgin Island Daily News* from the steps of the villa.

Back at the table, he unfolded the *Times* first. Then with dismay he read the headline on the right-hand side of the page. "Parker Bennett's Secretary Indicted as Co-

conspirator."

Eleanor didn't have a thing to do with it, he thought; not one single thing. Of course he could do nothing to help her but he was genuinely sorry for her. She had made it easy for him to rope in his early clients. He knew that she must have been questioned relentlessly by the FBI and SEC. Maybe with luck, if she took a lie detector test and passed, it would help her at her trial.

There had been only one instance in the thirteen years she had worked for him when he could have given himself away. It was when he dropped the cards out of his wallet and the British driver's license with the name "George Hawkins" was clearly visible. He didn't think that Eleanor had looked at the name and would remember it. But if she remembered the name and had recognized that it was not a US driver's license, it might help investigators narrow the search for him.

And if Sylvie was throwing around money at the rate she was demanding it of him, it would be a red flag for the Feds. He knew it had gotten around that he and Sylvie were involved romantically.

"Romantically." He spat out her name derisively. Stupidly, he was carrying the receipt for the dinghy and outboard motor he had bought to make his escape after ditching the sailboat. It listed his George Hawkins name, address in St. Thomas, and phone number. When he had stayed over at her apartment that last night, she must have gone through his wallet. He had been in St. Thomas only a few days when she called him on his cell and greeted him by saying, "Do I have the pleasure of speaking to Mr. George Hawkins?"

That had been the beginning of the blackmail.

Because she knew his new identity and where he was, he was not able to say no to what he knew would be a steady stream of requests for money. He had had to be very careful and do it in a way that would make the transfers appear legitimate if they were discovered by the FBI.

He had phoned his Swiss banker contact, the one who had helped him with so many delicate tasks. As usual, Adolph had come through.

Adolph had created a holding company in the name of Eduardo de la Marco, Sylvie's late husband. Each time he sent her money, Adolph first transferred it into the holding company, and then the holding company wired the payment to Countess de la Marco. If the payments to her were discovered, his hope was that investigators would mistakenly believe they were part of her settlement.

Parker unfolded the *Post* reluctantly, knowing that Eleanor's arrest would be headline news. It was worse than he expected. Pictures of him and Eleanor were side by side on the front page. The headline was "Parker Bennett Secretary Indicted."

The picture of Eleanor had been taken after she posted bond. Tears were running down her cheeks. She was clutching her husband Frank's hand as if she was afraid of falling.

She looks terrible, Parker thought with a twinge of sympathy. Then he studied his own picture.

It had been taken at a charity dinner where he was being honored. It had been enlarged, and as he studied it, Parker realized how thin his disguise really was. Seized with fear, he walked to the mirror hanging over the fireplace in the living room and held the paper near his face. He had the brown wig on. It was now a reflex for him to put it on after he showered, and of course, it did change his appearance, but not enough if anyone really studied him. He had already applied the putty on the sides of his nose. He was not wearing the sunglasses that he habitually wore outside the house, but with or without them, an acute observer might recognize him. He went back to the table. His second cup of coffee was no longer warm but he hardly noticed it.

Today the water was choppy and the weatherman on the radio had warned of a late-afternoon storm. It would be a good day for golfing. The Shallow Reef course he went to had become his favorite. Possibly because I get my lowest scores there, he acknowledged. I'll go there this morning, he decided. The thought of staying in the house and worrying all day was unacceptable.

When he arrived at the course at eleven o'clock, he was dismayed to see that Len Stacey, the acquaintance who had pestered him with questions about engineers in England whom he might have known, was there.

To his dismay, Stacey greeted him as though they were old friends. "George, just in time. We need you to complete a foursome. It will be you and me and the two guys we played with last time."

Four hours of him asking questions, Parker thought. "Oh, I'm only going to hit some practice balls today," he said, hoping his voice sounded disappointed.

"Oh, too bad," Stacey said. "How about we firm up a date later in the week?"

Parker knew he had been backed into a corner. There was no way he could refuse to set a date without displaying open rudeness that could draw attention to himself.

"Friday would be fine." I'll have to tell this guy that I'll be leaving, he thought, and how many questions will he ask about that? Then he realized that there was a copy of the *New York Post* on the counter next to where Stacey was standing. He noticed that after Stacey turned from him with a friendly wave, he picked up the paper, glanced at the front page, and then turned to look at him again.

22

On Wednesday morning, Lane reluctantly drove to meet the installation crew at Anne Bennett's town house. It was a gloomy day, overcast but not raining, not cold but with a chill in the air.

She had left in enough time to be sure to be there when the crew arrived at eleven. But when she rang the bell and Anne Bennett answered the door, Lane was surprised to see that she was still in pajamas.

"Oh, Mrs. Bennett, is this an inconvenient time for you to have the accessories installed in your bedroom?" she asked.

"No, of course not. Come in, Lane."

As Lane stepped into the foyer, Anne closed the door behind her quickly.

"I get cold so easily," she murmured. "I'll run upstairs and get dressed before the others get here. The coffeepot is on, so pour yourself a cup if you want it."

As Lane began to reply, Mrs. Bennett

turned and went up the stairs.

That poor woman is so distracted, Lane thought. I wonder if Parker's secretary being indicted is the cause, although Eric didn't even mention her when we had dinner. But of course her arrest is starting a new surge of publicity about the case. It has to be hurtful to see your husband's picture on the front page of newspapers and have him referred to as a crook.

Ten minutes later Alan Greene and two of his assistants arrived. Alan was the owner of the company that had made the bedspread, vanity skirt, and draperies and reupholstered the chaise and headboard. Usually he did not come himself for a job like this, but when Glady was involved, he always made it his business to oversee everything.

He greeted Lane with easy familiarity. "Hi, Lane. How's Her Imperial Majesty?"

"Doing fine, Alan."

"I'm so glad. This is the biggest rush job she ever handed us. Do you get to sign off on it?"

"Yes I do, so it had better be perfect."

They both laughed.

Lane remembered there had been a few occasions when Glady had vented her wrath on Alan. "Those are not the tassels I ordered for the pillows, Alan. Can't you get anything

131

straight?"

"Glady," Alan had said patiently, "you were between two samples and you chose this one. See where you signed for it?"

One of the things Lane loved about Alan was that he bested Glady at her own game. He made her sign a card for everything she ordered and would attach it to the swatch or sample tassel she chose.

With his helpers he started upstairs, but Lane stopped him.

"You'd better let me see if Mrs. Bennett is dressed," Lane said. "I'll check on her."

The bedroom door was open. Lane was shocked to see Anne Bennett lying on the unmade bed with her eyes closed.

"Mrs. Bennett, do you feel ill?" Lane asked, alarmed at the ghostly white pallor of the other woman's face.

Mrs. Bennett opened her eyes. "Oh, I'm all right. I'll go into one of the other bedrooms and rest there. Can you handle everything for me? I mean, if I have to sign an approval for the job, just do it for me."

"Of course."

Lane watched with concern as the older woman pulled herself up and slowly got to her feet. Impulsively she offered her arm and seemingly without noticing, Bennett took it. "I'll get dressed later," she said as she slowly walked down the hall.

"Of course," Lane answered soothingly. "I saw that you didn't drink your coffee. May I bring you up a fresh cup?"

"No, not now. Thank you." In the guest bedroom, she immediately lay down on the bed and sighed. "Please close the door, Lane," she said, her voice low and strained.

"Try to rest." Lane left the room quietly. She doesn't look well, she thought, alarmed. Maybe I should call Eric. She'd decide that later. She couldn't hold up Alan and his crew now.

An hour later the master bedroom had been transformed. The intense blue of the walls, broken by the white wainscoting, made a striking background for the white coverlet and blue bed skirt, which was the same color as the wall.

The draperies, valances, vanity skirt, and chaise complemented the blue and white theme with a colorful flower pattern.

The bedroom had become an inviting and charming chamber.

"Absolutely great," Lane enthused.

Alan smiled. "Tell Glady not to hit us with any more 'I want it yesterday' calls."

"I'll do that," she promised.

"On the other hand, don't tell her. I hear she's got Countess Sylvie de la Marco as a new client. I want to be part of that scene, so tell Glady it's always a pleasure to work on a tight schedule when it's for her."

"Is that the final message?"

"Sure, only you can throw in that she's the best interior designer I know and I'm proud to work for her." He paused. "That should do it."

It was nearly noon when Alan and his crew left. Lane was not sure what she should do. If Anne Bennett was sleeping, she did not want to disturb her. On the other hand, if she was as ill as she looked, it wouldn't be right to leave her alone.

She had to risk checking on her. With one last admiring glance at the transformed room, she walked down the hallway and knocked on the door of the other bedroom.

When she heard a weak, "Come in," Lane opened the door. Mrs. Bennett was fully dressed. She had obviously put on some makeup because the ghostly pallor was partially concealed. But Lane could see that her eyes seemed sunken and weary.

"I'd better get downstairs. If Eric can get away early from a meeting, he will come for lunch," Anne said, a little animation in her tone.

"How nice for you," Lane said sincerely. But there was one thing she knew for sure.

She did not want to run into Eric Bennett. "And I've got to be on my way," she added. "Glady is expecting me back in the office by one o'clock."

"Surely you can spare a half hour to have something to eat," Anne protested.

At that moment there was a brief ring of the doorbell and then the door opened.

As Lane had feared, it was Eric. He was wearing a trench coat with the collar turned up. His hair was tousled from the wind. He was carrying a bag of groceries. He looked at her, smiled, and said, "Hello, Lane. Did Katie get my letter?"

"Yes she did. That was so nice of you."

"Does she know how to make oatmeal cookies?"

"She does now. And I must be on my way."

"You can't be. I brought in lunch for the three of us. You'll be out of here in forty-five minutes. I promise, because I have to leave by then too."

Anne Bennett was looking at her expectantly. "Please stay, Lane. I was looking forward to visiting with you."

Lane remembered Glady's warning, then brushed it aside. "I'd love to stay," she said. "What can I do to help?"

"Nothing," Eric said promptly. "You and Mother talk to me and I'll get everything ready. I bought chicken noodle soup and had them make up a small assortment of sandwiches," Eric announced as they went into the dinette. "How does that sound, Mom?"

"It sounds good to me, dear."

Lane saw that Anne Bennett had perceptibly brightened since Eric came in.

"How's Glady Harper?" was Anne's first question as she and Lane got settled at the table.

"Glady is Glady," Lane said, then added, "a perfectionist, as you know, very smart, and underneath her intimidating exterior, a very nice person."

"I certainly appreciate how kind she has been to me," Anne said quietly. "I don't know any other decorator who not only would select the furniture but also redo my bedroom." She looked at Eric, who was putting a bowl of soup on the table. "Don't you agree, Eric?"

"In a way I do, Mother," Eric said. "On the other hand, she made so much money when she decorated our house ten years ago that I don't think you need to go overboard being grateful to her."

The words seemed harsh to Lane, but they were said in a gentle voice, and she could see the affection in Eric's eyes as he

136

looked at his mother.

The soup was delicious and a reminder that she had slept a little later this morning and had been behind schedule giving Katie breakfast. When Bettina had arrived to walk Katie to preschool, she had not yet brushed her hair and put on the little makeup she habitually wore to work. Because she was coming out here, she had driven her car and parked near the office. In the car, when she stopped for a red light, she had put on some blush and twisted her hair and fastened it up with a comb, but she knew it was not the best hairdressing job.

Eric made some coffee and Lane said, "I'm afraid I don't have time for more than a few sips before I leave."

"I so enjoyed visiting with you," Anne said, "and Eric has told me about your adorable little girl."

"She's pretty special," Lane agreed. "I have to admit that. I'll be back," she said, changing the subject. "I want to take the small pillows on the couch and chairs in the living room. They look a bit tired and it will be very easy for us to replace them."

And what will Glady have to say about that? she wondered, and then stood up.

"Glady will be at the window looking for me. I really have to go. I'll collect the pillows and be on my way."

"I'll take them out to your car," Eric said.

Lane could have bitten her tongue. This meant they would be alone for a few moments and she didn't want that. Being with him made her realize how intensely she had hoped that he would call her for another dinner date.

After he had put the pillows in the backseat of the car, he interrupted her quick "Thanks, Eric," as she turned the ignition key.

"Lane," he said with his eyes focused intently on her face. "You must have realized how very much I enjoyed having dinner with you."

"It was very pleasant," she agreed evasively. "And now I really have to be off."

"Lane, it was more than very pleasant. It was special, and I think you felt that too. I can't tell you how many times I turned on my phone to call you and then turned it off again."

"Why did you do that?" she asked, even though she instinctively knew the answer.

"I didn't call you because I'm Eric Bennett, son of Parker Bennett, master crook. You certainly have seen the headlines this past week. My father's secretary has been indicted. That's started a rehash of the case. Poor Eleanor is no more a thief than I am. You must have noticed that my mother looked pretty pale today. She's been reading all that stuff in the tabloids about my father's affairs, especially with Countess de la Marco. It's tearing her apart."

He paused. "Lane, I'll say it straight. The paparazzi have me in their crosshairs. If you go out to dinner with me, you may end up in the gossip columns. You're the stepdaughter of a powerful columnist who hates my guts."

"And I'm the daughter of a congressman who absolutely despised guilt by association," Lane said crisply. "Eric, I get the message that you want to have dinner with me. How about Saturday night at eight o'clock?"

For an answer, Eric leaned in the car and kissed her forehead. "Saturday at eight," he said. "You say that Katie is making oatmeal cookies now. Put my order in for two."

"I shall."

As she backed the car out of the driveway, she could see in the rearview mirror that Tony Russo was waiting to pull his car into the driveway. She waved as she passed him.

As Jon waved back, she could not know that he was thinking, How could she get involved with that lowlife? Is she out of her mind?

23

On Wednesday afternoon Sean Cunningham drove up the West Side Highway to visit Eleanor Becker in Yonkers, New York. It was a relatively short distance. No traffic, about forty minutes, Sean thought. Usual traffic, an hour and a quarter.

Actually he liked driving and used the time in the car to go over in his mind the best way he could help Eleanor through her ordeal. There was not a question in his mind that a jury would find her guilty as a co-conspirator to Parker Bennett. That meant she might be sentenced to as little as five years or as much as fifteen or even longer.

It was impossible that Parker Bennett committed the theft without help, and she was the most likely suspect. It should have been Parker's son, Sean thought, but they haven't a shred of evidence against him.

The Becker house was only fifteen minutes from the Yonkers exit off the Saw Mill River

Parkway. It was on a street with older, well-kept homes. The last time he had been here the trees had been abundant with leaves that had softened the fact that Eleanor and Frank's house badly needed a paint job.

Now there were dead leaves scattered on the lawn and he could see that the gutters were overflowing with them.

Shaking his head, he rang the bell. The door was opened immediately. Eleanor was almost unrecognizable. The sweater and slacks she was wearing hung off her gaunt frame. Her hair was pure white and held back from her face with bobby pins. She was a shadow of the woman he had seen six months ago.

"Come in, Sean," she said. "Come in." Tears began to spill from her eyes. "It's so nice of you to come. Most people are avoiding me. Remember in the Bible, the lepers had to shout 'Unclean, unclean,' if anyone came near them?"

"Yes I do," Sean said, "but, Eleanor, you are not unclean and you know it."

"I do know it, and what good does that do me?"

She led the way into the small den where Frank was sitting in a reclining chair. "Hi, doctor, good of you to come."

His voice sounded cheerful but Sean was

sure it was a false bravado for Eleanor's benefit. How could it be anything else? he asked himself.

He got straight to the point. "I've been trying to decide how I can help you," he told them.

"There is no way to help me," Eleanor said, dabbing at her eyes.

"Eleanor, I want you to think hard. It's obvious Parker had this scheme going for the entire thirteen years his fund existed. What I want is for you to go over it in your mind and see if you can remember any time that you felt something seemed odd to you. I know it's asking a lot, but it's hard to believe that at least once in that time Parker didn't slip in some way."

Eleanor shook her head. "I don't think so. I really don't."

Sean stayed for an hour and had a cup of tea with them. He could see that the realization that he absolutely believed in Eleanor's innocence was a comfort to both of them.

But being a comfort to them isn't the same as helping them, he thought as he drove home in the gloomy, cloud-filled afternoon that was a reflection of his state of mind.

24

At 26 Federal Plaza Rudy Schell stared in frustration at the newspapers on his desk. Besides the ones from New York, there were the *Washington Post,* the *Chicago Tribune,* the *Los Angeles Times,* and the *San Francisco Examiner.*

On every front page there was a picture of Parker Bennett and Eleanor Becker.

Rudy had interviewed Becker a half dozen times and had tried every trick in the book to trip her up on her story.

Every instinct told him that she was not involved in the fraud. He had expressed his opinion to the prosecutor, who did not agree and had gone to the grand jury to get an indictment. She may be dumb, he thought, but she's not a crook.

He corrected himself. She may not be dumb, but she sure is naïve if she never for one minute wondered about Bennett's consistently high annual returns to the investors.

The two people who might be in touch with Parker Bennett if he was still alive were his son, Eric, and his girlfriend, Sally Chico, alias Countess Sylvie de la Marco.

They had been investigated up and down and no agency had been able to pin anything on them. Of course it was entirely possible, even probable, that they had unregistered prepaid phones that could not be traced. Yesterday there had been an item in one of the gossip columns saying that famed interior decorator Glady Harper was redecorating the countess's duplex.

That meant she would be in and out of the apartment frequently. Would it work for him to ask Harper to keep her eyes and ears open when she was there? Would she cooperate with them, or have some kind of loyalty to her client and tell her that she had been approached by the FBI to spy on her? He would have to weigh the decision.

Now to figure out who could keep tabs on Eric Bennett.

That would be harder. As far as any investigator could see, he had been something of a lone wolf since the scandal broke. Hard to tell if it was his choice to withdraw from the University Club and the Racquet and Tennis Club, or if it had been suggested to him that it would be appropriate for him to withdraw. They had gotten permission to wire his mother's town house in the hope that she or Eric might say something that would help them find Parker Bennett.

Rudy had Googled Glady Harper. There were volumes about her. She had redecorated the second floor of the White House, where the presidential family lived. Famously known for her blunt appraisals, she had said of the painting of Dolley Madison's sister on the wall of the Queen's Bedroom, "That woman was so homely the queen must have turned it around on the wall at night."

Schell noted that she had also redecorated Blair House, where visiting royalty now stayed during a state visit, and had won any number of awards in interior design.

Ten years ago, Harper had decorated the baronial mansion of Parker Bennett in Greenwich. Now she was decorating the apartment of Countess Sylvie de la Marco in Manhattan. It was common knowledge that the countess had had a long-running affair with Parker Bennett.

Schell had to wonder: was she in touch with him now?

25

Countess Sylvie de la Marco had been born with the survival instinct of her hardscrabble background. That was what had transformed her from Sally Chico of Staten Island to the holder of a title and a luxury apartment on Fifth Avenue. But now that background was giving her a warning, and it had to do with Parker.

Of course people had guessed that for many years she and Parker had been an item even though they had been very discreet about their affair. In public they only went out in a group. From time to time there had been blind items about it: "Which financier was holding hands under the table at Le Cirque with what titled socialite?"

She had always made it her business to attend social events with some divorced male celebrities to further keep talk about Parker and her down.

But now, since Parker's secretary had been

146

indicted, not only the gossip columns but even the news reports were openly stating that she and Parker were alleged to have been involved with each other for years.

Sylvie knew that she had been under close scrutiny ever since Parker had disappeared. But the fact that the de la Marco family was known to be worth a fortune had been in her favor. The prenup records were sealed, so no one knew how much she had gotten from Eduardo's estate. She had always been careful about discussing it.

When she had a couple of scotches, she had complained to a few close friends that she could kick herself for signing a prenup that only gave her lifetime use of the apartment, maintenance of it, and a monthly allowance.

Of course she had never intended that she wouldn't get more. She had been sure that she would have been able to get Eduardo to tear up the prenup, but that had not happened.

Another bone of contention was that in their four-year marriage, she could never get Eduardo to let her redecorate. Then when he died, the decorator she got made no suggestions, just followed her instructions. Everything was all wrong, Sylvie admitted to herself. That's why the columnists call it the brass cage. The decorator's only virtue was that she was cheap.

But had it been stupid to start a five-million-dollar renovation now? Parker had always been generous, but he had been furious when he realized that she had gone through his wallet and found the receipt in the name of George Hawkins for the dinghy and outboard motor as well as the address and phone number in St. Thomas. She had made a copy of it. Just a hunch, she thought, but boy did it work out!

Parker disappeared the next day. A week later she had tried the phone number and reached him.

It amused her that he almost dropped dead when she called him.

He had taken off with five billion dollars. The money she had requested him to send was a drop in the bucket compared with what he had. So why had he sounded so angry when she called him and asked for more money last week?

He had never been cheap with her. Every piece of jewelry she wore had been a gift from Parker. In the prenup she had also agreed that any de la Marco gems Eduardo gave her were to be returned to the family after his death.

Once the interior decorating was finished, she would take it easy on Parker.

Sylvie made that decision sitting in a satin robe in the library, as she was picking at the breakfast that the butler, Robert, had placed before her.

She had sipped the chilled fresh orange juice and had a few bites of the fruit. But it was the coffee she really wanted. Robert had poured the first cup. She could have rung the bell that would have sent him scurrying from wherever he was to serve her, but instead she lifted the silver coffeepot and poured the second cup herself.

It was good to have a staff attending to her 24/7. Robert also served as her chauffeur in the Mercedes S500. Much as she wanted to have a Rolls, she had listened to Parker's warning, "Sylvie, stay under the radar."

Mrs. Carson, the housekeeper, was from the old school, as Parker used to say about her. "Yes, ma'am." "No, ma'am." She was quiet and diligent. Age sixty to one hundred, as Parker used to put it. But of course Mrs. Carson only saw him when she had a dinner party for six or more people.

The private entrance from the street and private elevator ensured Parker's visits alone with her were discreet. Neither Mrs. Carson nor Carla, the maid, nor Robert stayed overnight. If Parker was coming for dinner or to stay over, he arrived after they left and was out in the morning before they arrived. Chez Francis, the five-star restaurant on the lobby floor, would send up dinner and then remove it later.

Parker would wait in the library with the door closed when the restaurant service arrived and was taken away. So the staff never could be sure if the same person was her frequent guest. But now their affair was out for one and all to see — including the federal government. If they didn't know about it before, they knew about it now.

She would have to be very careful. She would dismiss any questions about her relationship with Parker as meaningless gossip. She would not call him for more money until she needed to pay Glady Harper more.

But she shouldn't be so worried. Parker must have seen those newspapers too. And he certainly knew that if promised immunity from prosecution, she could turn him in and collect the considerable reward for information leading to his apprehension. She might have to remind him of that.

There was a light tap on the library door, followed by Robert's opening it.

"Ms. Harper is here, Countess," he announced. "Shall I send her in?"

"That won't be necessary. Let her go ahead with anything she plans to do today. Tell her if she has any specific questions for me, I will receive her after I am dressed."

That will put her in her place, Sylvie thought with satisfaction. She may be a good decorator, but I'm the one paying the bills and I don't need to put up with her nasty little comments.

26

The bell rang at promptly eight o'clock on Saturday evening. Before Lane could stop her, with a whoop of delight, Katie ran to open the door.

"Katie, are you the official greeter?" Eric Bennett asked with a smile.

"I made you two oatmeal cookies. One of them has raisins in it and the other one has nuts. I didn't know which one you liked best," Katie said happily.

"I like them just the same."

Lane was halfway across the living room. "Please come in, Eric. And may I say that you certainly are a diplomat." She was smiling, but her glance at Katie's face had been disquieting. Katie looked absolutely radiant.

The other day over dinner she had said, "Grace told me that I must have done something bad because my father doesn't come to see me."

"Katie, you know that your daddy and I

were in a very bad accident. He was hurt so badly that he died. Now he's with my daddy in heaven."

It was the story she had always told Katie, but the other night had been different. Katie had started to cry.

"I don't want my daddy to be in heaven. I want him to be here with me just like the other kids."

The psychologist she talked with occasionally had warned her that that could happen. But he hadn't needed to warn her. Her own heart had ached for a father she adored. Katie had never known a father's embrace.

There was a void, and Katie was trying to fill it because Eric Bennett had been nice to her.

I have to be careful, Lane thought. Katie sensed that when I told her Eric was coming I was happy. She's playing "follow the leader."

"Hello, Eric," she said as she struggled to sound friendly but not too much so.

There was an amused look in his eyes, as though he could read her thoughts. "Good to be with you two beautiful ladies," he said, and then looked across the room at Wilma Potters, who was sitting on the couch in the living room. "Three beautiful ladies," he

153

corrected himself.

Katie was tugging at his hand. "I'll show you the cookies but Mommy said you don't have to eat one until after dinner."

"That's what I'll do then."

Five minutes later she and Eric were downstairs on the sidewalk and Eric was signaling for a cab. When one pulled up, he said, "There's a great new steakhouse in the Village. Sound all right to you?"

Lane hesitated. Was this one of those hot places where the paparazzi might be lurking? Eric had warned her that he was becoming a target for them. But if she asked him that, it would only sound as though she didn't want to be photographed with him.

"Sounds great," she said.

To her relief, no photographers were hanging around outside of the restaurant. Inside, the maître d' led them to a quiet table. Lane began to relax.

Over a cocktail Eric kept the conversation safe. He told her how much his mother enjoyed her company and how delighted she was with the way her bedroom now looked.

"You know," he said, "I honestly think she's going to be really happy in the town house. I don't believe she was ever really comfortable in Greenwich in that over-the-top mansion. My father took to the lifestyle

154

like a duck to water but my mother was always somewhat insecure."

Lane had hoped that Eric would steer clear of the subject of his father, but maybe that was impossible. She saw Eric suddenly tense and she was sure that he'd had the same thought.

His voice sounded rueful when he said, "All roads lead to Rome, it seems. I'm sorry I brought up my father's name. I want to say something more on the subject and then get off it. Last Friday I went to visit Patrick Adams. He runs a firm very much like the one Mayor Giuliani created. It's about top-drawer security and investigating to find out everything about someone's background. Adams is known as someone who can ferret out the truth, whatever it is."

"Why did you go to see him?" Lane asked.

"Because if there is any conceivable way to clear my name, I want to do it. He warned me that if he found out that I had been involved in the theft, he would turn me over to the FBI. Quite frankly it will cost me every nickel that I don't need for living expenses, but it will be worth it."

Eric hesitated, then reached over the table and placed his hand over hers. "Lane, I want my future. As far as I am able I want to be exonerated by public opinion in that

155

terrible theft. Frankly if my father is still alive, I hope he's caught. If he is, I know that he will tell the world that I had nothing to do with the disappearance of that money."

His hand was still on hers. Lane liked the feel of it there. Ken used to touch her hand like that as they toasted each other — a ritual for them when they went to a restaurant and even at home.

Ken, she thought longingly.

But it was not Ken who was looking at her lovingly.

What is happening to me? Am I like Katie, so eager to fill a void in my life that the first time I feel myself responding to an attractive man I throw aside discretion?

Be careful, she warned herself as she reluctantly withdrew her hand from his firm grasp.

27

On Sunday morning Anne Bennett went to the ten o'clock Mass at the Church of the Immaculate Conception, then stopped at the drugstore to pick up some Tylenol. It was just a precaution. She no longer had the blinding migraine headaches that used to paralyze her regularly.

She was also trying to stop taking the anti-depressant pills that the doctor had prescribed to her.

The last few days had been terrible, she admitted to herself. Eric had told her not to read the newspapers, but how could she try to ignore them since they carried the story of Eleanor's indictment?

That poor woman, Anne thought for the hundredth time as she paid for the Tylenol and left the pharmacy. Should I call her? Would she even want to hear from me? I simply don't know. On the way home, out of curiosity, she drove past the restaurant that her neighbor, Tony Russo, was in the process of building. It was going to be large, she thought. He must be investing a great deal of money in it.

Money. The word — an automatic segue to Parker. As she drove home, the brightness of the sun caused her to lower the visor, and that caused her to glance into the rearview mirror.

Was she wrong or was that old black Ford the same car that had been parked next to hers at the drugstore?

Not that again, she thought with a sinking heart. For a long time after Parker's disappearance, she knew she had been followed around not only by government agents but also by some attention-seeking nobodies who would then post her picture on the Internet.

Was that starting again?

She deliberately steered the car on an indirect route to the town house but could see that she was still being followed.

Suddenly nervous, she drove more quickly until she turned into her driveway, and then braked sharply because Tony Russo was walking up it. She waited to let him pass but he tapped on her window. She opened it, suddenly grateful for his presence.

"I was just going to say good morning,"

Russo said, then looked at her closely. "Are you okay, Mrs. Bennett? You came in so fast, I wondered if you were upset."

Anne liked her new neighbor. Eric had warned her to watch every word she uttered but she could not resist saying, "I am a bit flustered. I think I was followed home just now."

Instantly aware, Tony asked, "What kind of car was following you?"

His eyes looked past her at the street as she said, "A really old black Ford."

As she spoke, Tony could see a tired-looking black Ford drive past the town house.

Anne decided to be frank with him. "Tony, if you don't already know, Parker Bennett is my husband and I've been followed around several times since his disappearance. I had hoped it was over but I guess it isn't." She closed the window without waiting for him to answer and pulled forward into her garage.

Jon went straight into his own town house. He immediately made a call and asked a question. "Are you guys putting a tail on Anne Bennett?" As he had expected, the answer was no.

He broke the connection and immediately punched in another number.

28

On Saturday morning, Parker Bennett decided that he absolutely could not put up with more of Len Stacey's inane chatter on the golf course today.

It was perfect sailing weather, sunny, a slight breeze, the kind of day that was made for him to go out on his boat. Especially since it had been raining for the last three days.

Trying to sound hoarse and forcing a cough, he phoned his unwanted golfing partner. "Len, this is a real disappointment. I was looking forward to taking your money today. But I feel really lousy. I'm going back to bed. Didn't sleep last night so I'm turning off the phone."

"Ah, come on, George. I've been looking forward to our rematch," Len replied.

His grating laugh put Parker's teeth on edge. Before he could respond Len added, "And you know what? I planned to run a contest in the locker room today. I was going to ask the guys in our foursome, 'Who looks like Parker Bennett?' I bet at least one of them votes that you look like him."

"Like *who*?" Parker said as the fingers holding his cell phone went numb.

"Oh come on. Parker Bennett, the big crook. He's been all over the papers this last week."

"Oh sure, I know who he is," Bennett answered. "But you think I look like him?" As he spoke he realized that he had dropped the low, cough-enhanced tone in his voice.

"Hey, don't be touchy," Len said. "I'm just kidding. Forget it. It was a lousy idea."

"Yes it was." Bennett coughed, a raspy sound. "If you want to say I look like Donald Trump that's okay." He attempted a laugh. "All right, sorry to miss you today. Play well."

When he disconnected, Bennett realized that his palms were so damp that the phone almost slipped out of his grasp. He had been right. That idiot had been comparing him with the pictures on the front page of the *Post.*

Wait a minute, he warned himself. Don't panic again. That would destroy you. You've been known around here for fifteen years. You have an impeccable British accent.

Even if he sees a resemblance, he's not smart enough to think there is any chance that I am Parker Bennett. Taking some consolation in that probability, Parker went down to the dock and got into the boat. Five minutes later, the sails unfurled, he was out on the water.

Over the past two years he had sometimes wondered what would happen if he got caught. But of course he knew what would happen. He would go to prison for the rest of his life. He was seventy-two years old now, but his family was long-lived. Although his father had smoked himself to death at a young age, his grandfather and his uncles had lived until their early nineties. At least twenty years in prison, he thought. No way.

And it didn't have to happen. Once he got the number of the Swiss account, he'd be home free. He had put in a bid on the villa outside Geneva he had seen on the Internet. It was the right size for him and newly refurbished.

He had begun to miss Anne. Funny that for the past two years he'd hardly thought of her. But the other night he had dreamed of her. It had been a vivid dream. She was holding the music box and dancing. She always had a fixation about that music box. It was probably the cheapest gift he ever gave her. And of course now it was worth five billion dollars, less about fifteen million.

Deep in reverie, Parker had not noticed that the wind had become brisk and one of the sudden Caribbean storms was imminent. He turned the boat to head back to shore, but in minutes the sea was turbulent and the rain blinding. At one point the boat heeled so much to one side that his hand touched the water. If he hadn't let out the mainsail the boat would have turned over. Experienced though he was, when he finally got to shore and raced through pelting rain to the house Parker was gasping for breath, and keenly aware that he had been lucky to make it back safely.

The phone rang. The caller ID showed it was that miserable pest Len. On the other hand, he was lucky that he was here to answer it. After all his show of having a heavy cold, he lowered his voice, trying to give it a raspy sound.

"Hello, George. Just wanted to see how you're doing, old buddy."

"Oh, that's thoughtful of you." Parker forced a pleasant tone into his voice. "I'm over the worst of it."

"That's good. I have to apologize about saying you look like Parker Bennett. No one in our foursome agreed with me."

"Oh, then you *did* have your guess-who game?"

"Just between the four of us. No one guessed who. In fact Dewayne thought you look like Mayor de Blasio of New York." Once again Len's grating laugh pounded like drums in Parker's ears. He could feel a net closing around him. It was happening suddenly, just as the storm had come up so suddenly.

What should he do?

29

As Ranger drove past Anne Bennett's, he decided that he had to be careful. He didn't want anyone to notice his car. But of course it would be noticeable. It was twelve years old now and had been secondhand when Judy and he bought it. Someone had dented the front fender in the parking lot of the supermarket a few months ago. No question, if you saw it, you'd remember it.

This was the second time he had driven past the town house where Parker Bennett's wife lived. Pretty nice, he thought. A lot nicer than any place he and Judy had ever lived. Oh, maybe it wasn't good enough for Bennett's wife. She was used to that fancy place in Connecticut. He'd seen pictures of it.

The first time he went by Anne Bennett's place in New Jersey had been a couple of days ago. He had parked down the street. Parker Bennett's son, Eric, had been there in the driveway. There was a good-looking woman, young, maybe late twenties, with him. Eric put something in her car and then leaned into the driver's window. Ranger was sure that he was kissing the woman.

Today he had followed Anne Bennett to church. He'd even gone into the Mass and sat in the last row. He knew he didn't look out of place. His jeans weren't worn out and Judy had bought his jacket for him at a secondhand store two years ago, just before Bennett disappeared. She had been passing the store and saw it in the window. He remembered how hard she had laughed when she told him about the lettering "TP" on the breast pocket. "Oh, Ranger, I asked the clerk if those letters stood for 'Turnpike Authority.' That guy put on a real snooty look and said it stood for 'Trinity-Pawling.' He said that it was a really classy boarding school for boys."

We drove an old car. Sometimes I wore secondhand clothes so that we could save to buy the condo in Florida — all cash, he thought. Probably everyone at Mass from around here would know this was a jacket that meant he had gone to a high-class school.

He had followed Anne Bennett into the drugstore and down the aisle, where he watched as she bought Tylenol. He hoped she had a headache. He hoped that she and her son and her son's girlfriend all had the worst headaches that anyone in the world had ever had.

There wasn't much traffic, and before he knew it he was almost at the entrance of the Lincoln Tunnel. He could be home in half an hour. But what good would that do him? Home was that three-room apartment that Judy had always kept so nice. She liked to keep it no higher than sixty-eight degrees but always turned the thermostat up when he was due home. She understood that after being out in the cold all day, it was so good to feel the warmth the minute he opened the door.

She knew that he was always hungry when he got home, so dinner was always ready for him. The warmth and the good smells coming from the kitchen — Ranger remembered them so keenly that as he drove through the Lincoln Tunnel he felt that he was experiencing them again.

Parker Bennett's wife was living in a nice house in a nice town. Eric Bennett was kissing his pretty girlfriend. And he was going home to an empty apartment. Ranger clasped his hand around the vial of Judy's ashes that he wore around his neck.

"Judy," he said aloud. "I know you won't want me to do it but I have to. Please understand."

He watched the E-Z Pass register as he entered the tunnel.

Lots of people think that crook Parker Bennett isn't dead. They think he let that fancy sailboat of his get washed up on shore to make people think he had killed himself.

But maybe he didn't. What would it be like for Bennett to read somewhere that his wife and son had been killed?

Ranger remembered the pretty woman Eric Bennett had been kissing. If she's around when it happens, so much the better. He's probably spending our money on her too. If she happens to be there when I shoot Anne Bennett and her son, it'll be just her hard luck.

He had to buy a gun. He didn't think it would be hard to get his hands on one. He was always reading in the newspapers about that section of the Bronx where gang members sold them.

There was no rush. Just planning what he would do felt good. It almost felt like walking into the apartment when it was warm and he was smelling something good cooking on the stove.

What was it Judy used to say? Oh yes.

"Oh, Ranger, I'm looking forward to the move to Florida so much. They say that anticipation may be more enjoyable than when something actually happens. Do you think that could be true?"

I'll find out, Ranger thought as he reached his street and began the usual search for a parking spot.

30

Patrick Adams headed a team of four investigators, men who, as he put it, could track down a leaf in a windstorm. On Monday morning he called them to a meeting in his office.

"I see why Eric Bennett is so anxious to clear his name," he said. "There's a picture of him in the *Post* holding hands with Lane Harmon. She's the daughter of the late Congressman Gregory Harmon and the widow of Kenneth Kurner, the designer. She's also the stepdaughter of Dwight Crowley, the columnist who happens to think that Eric Bennett is involved with his father in the fraud and says so in every other column."

"That should make for a nice family Thanksgiving," Joel Weber, one of the investigators, drawled. Joel, the most recently hired of the investigators, was a former FBI agent who had gotten bored in retirement and then connected with the firm. At fifty-six, the same age as Pat Adams, and a former supervisor in the FBI, he had become a valued addition to the firm. What Pat especially liked was that Joel never for a moment tried to use his former position to throw his weight around in the office.

Pat Adams was behind his desk, the other four in a semicircle in front of it. Pat fixed his eyes on Joel, taking in with approval the fact that Joel's wry comments usually were the basis for an interesting suggestion about how to move the investigation forward.

"What are you thinking, Joel?" he asked.

"I'm wondering if Dwight Crowley has an ax to grind that he hasn't written about in public. I'd like to pursue that. I mean, the guy has an almost unreasonable hatred of Eric Bennett. The FBI, the Attorney General's office, and the Federal Investigative Regional Authority can't find one scrap of evidence against Eric Bennett, yet Crowley has said in his columns that the word 'alleged' doesn't pertain to Eric Bennett. Bennett could sue him for that. Now, maybe he hasn't because he doesn't want any more publicity. Or maybe Crowley has something on him that hasn't been disclosed so far."

Pat Adams was about to say that Joel

should ferret out more information on that possibility but before he could speak, Joel said, "And one more thing," as he took off his round horn-rimmed glasses, blew on them, wiped them dry, and replaced them.

"I said a few words to Eric Bennett in the reception room the other morning," he continued. "You know what I thought when I met him?"

Pat Adams and the other three investigators knew it was a rhetorical question.

"My mother was paranoid about anything she bought in the fish store," Joel told them, his voice conversational. "No matter how nice a piece of fish looked, she brought it up to her nose and gave it the sniff test. She could tell in a heartbeat if it was starting to turn."

He concluded, "I have my mother's acute sense of smell. When I was talking to Eric Bennett here the other day I gave him the sniff test and he failed it. I'd like to have the okay to find out why Dwight Crowley is so vehement about him. I also want to dig deep into Eric Bennett's background and see if I can find out anything about him that hasn't been dug up so far."

31

"Lie down with the dogs and get up with the fleas," was Glady's tart greeting to Lane on Monday morning.

Taken aback, Lane asked, "Glady, what in the name of God are you talking about?"

Glady grabbed the newspaper on her desk and shoved it across the table. "I'm talking about you being all lovey-dovey with Eric Bennett. I know you read the *Post* every day, I'm surprised you haven't seen it."

"Yes, I do, but certainly not in the morning when I have to get Katie and myself out," Lane said heatedly as she reached for the paper. It was turned to the gossip page. Dismayed, she saw a good-sized picture of herself with Eric Bennett. Whoever the photographer was, he or she had caught the moment when Eric's hand was covering hers and they were smiling at each other.

Her cheeks burning, Lane laid the paper back on Glady's desk. "That was the single moment when Eric happened to touch my hand," she said defensively.

"I believe you," Glady said. "In fact I wouldn't be surprised if Bennett paid someone to take that shot. Maybe it's even his version of a thumb in the eye to your stepfather."

"Glady, don't you see that this is exactly what Eric has been living under for two years now? No one can find a shred of evidence to tie him to that fraud, but everyone has decided that he was part of it. Don't you see how unfair that is? And I don't care what Dwight Crowley thinks. He's my mother's husband, but he's not my father. I was starting college the month my mother married him. I try to stay away from him. I time my visits to my mother when I know he's out giving speeches about how to run the world."

Even as she spoke Lane realized that Glady had brought up something that she never liked to admit even to herself. It was not just that she was uncomfortable around Dwight. She actively disliked him and knew that was the reason why she went to Washington so seldom, and why her relationship with her mother was so strained.

"Lane, it's none of my business if you are

seeing Eric Bennett. I think you're making a big mistake to let yourself get involved with him, but that's the end of my talking about it. I will tell you that I hate to think that the money Countess La-di-dah is paying me is coming from the money Parker Bennett stole. But you yourself saw the way the minute I told her how much my bill would be, she had to make an important phone call."

Without answering, Lane went to her own office, sat at the desk, and pressed her fingers against her temples. I'm not thinking straight, she acknowledged to herself. I *did* enjoy going to dinner with him.

We got back at ten thirty but Katie was still wide awake. The minute she heard our voices, she came rushing out to make sure Eric didn't forget the cookies she baked for him.

She wants to be like the other kids. She wants to have a father. Oh sure, many of them have divorced parents, but it's not the same as having to look at Daddy's picture and only hearing about him.

How long will it be before Dwight and my mother see the photo of me with Eric Bennett? Dwight glances through a heap of newspapers every day from all over the country as well as the London *Times*. He's not going to miss seeing that picture, and if he does someone will surely bring it to his attention.

What should I do? Either I believe Eric is innocent or I do not.

And I do.

But if I have dinner with Eric from time to time, how do I protect Katie? She thought of the moment Eric's hand had touched hers, of the fleeting good-night kiss on her lips that she could still feel. Let's face it, she thought, if that spark between us develops, *really* develops, would I want Eric's reputation, as the public sees it, to touch my life and Katie's?

But if I believe that Eric is innocent, as I wholeheartedly do, am I a coward for wondering if I would want to live with that situation?

Maybe I'll figure out an answer soon, she thought, but I don't have it now. But there was one thing she had to do. She dialed her mother at the antique shop.

Her mother's subdued, "Hello, Lane," told her that she and Dwight had seen the photo. "Look, Mom," Lane began, but her mother interrupted her.

"Lane, you don't have to convince me. I hope that if you learned one thing from me or about your father, it's that we both believe in 'innocent until proven guilty.' If Eric Bennett had nothing to do with his father's crime, he's as innocent a victim as those poor people who lost so much money."

"Thanks, Mom. I didn't know what you'd say. Now, how about Dwight, or should I dare ask?"

"Lane, my husband has never tried to influence me in any way regarding his belief that Eric Bennett was involved in his father's treachery."

"What did he say about the picture?" Lane demanded.

"He said he is aware that you have always been hostile to him, which makes him sad. He said, and I'll give you his exact words: 'Lane's father must be turning over in his grave at the thought that his daughter is dating that lowlife swine.' "

32

Eleanor Becker tried desperately to follow Dr. Sean Cunningham's advice and recall any incident in Parker Bennett's office that struck her as unusual.

Nothing, she thought, absolutely nothing. She knew she had a fairly good memory and asked Frank to talk to her about what they had discussed over the years. Of course at night she had chatted with him about the people who came and went. Maybe there was something that she could put her finger on?

Long ago something *did* happen that struck her as odd, but why couldn't she remember it?

Frank's diabetes was getting worse. His sugar level often reached alarming numbers. He's going to kill himself worrying about me, she thought. But what can I do about it?

It had been fifteen years now since Parker

Bennett, one of the top fund managers in the firm where they both worked, had told her that he wanted to take her out for a quiet lunch. "Not one of my usual places," he'd said with a "just between us" nod. "I have a business proposition for you."

She had known immediately what he meant. There had been speculation in the office that Bennett was probably going into business for himself at some point. Most of the smartest investment managers did that. Some of them made a lot of money and some of them opened their own hedge funds, made the wrong bet, and lost their shirt.

She remembered one of the managers who left them and made piles of money, then lost most of it because of the position he had taken trading oil. The joke around the stock market was that his wife was furious. He had promised her that he would put one hundred million dollars aside, just in case there was a sudden drastic change in the market. He hadn't done that, and now they only had their ten-million-dollar house to fall back on.

One hundred million dollars as a backup. For some reason that story kept rolling around in Eleanor's mind.

The place where Parker Bennett met her

for lunch was Neary's on Fifty-Seventh Street. Actually, she had been there before, a half dozen times at least. You never knew who you'd see there at night — high-ranking clergy, congressmen, business leaders, and so on. But lunch was quieter.

That was when Parker made his offer. "Eleanor, I'm going to leave the office and open my own place," he said. "I want you to come work for me."

The salary he had offered was more than generous. "And you'll be very pleased with your Christmas bonus," he had promised.

She would have leaped to say yes immediately, but then, when he told her the kind of investment firm he was planning, she was absolutely sure that he was not only a wonderful businessman but also a philanthropist.

"Eleanor," he had said, "we all know that people with real money are sophisticated, and when they do their financial planning they always have stocks and bonds in their portfolio."

Eleanor remembered how distinguished Parker Bennett had looked, and how he had looked her squarely in the eye as he sipped a glass of chardonnay.

"Eleanor," he said, "I came from nothing. My father was a mail carrier. My mother was a sales clerk at Abraham and Straus. It has been on my mind for years to help ordinary middle-class and lower-middle-class people like them, who are scrupulously putting aside a little money every month, to have a chance to get a decent return, while avoiding overly risky investments."

Then he outlined his plan, Eleanor thought bitterly. He would create a cozy, homelike atmosphere because, as he put it, "The little folks are easily intimidated, and we'll reach them by subscribing to a lot of local newspapers and writing to congratulate people who were given an award or celebrated an anniversary."

They called me the "tea and cookies lady," Eleanor remembered with hot shame. I fell for his plans hook, line, and sinker, and looked up to Parker Bennett as if he was the savior of mankind.

And now I may go to prison for my stupidity.

But there was something, there was something, there was something . . .

A week later, after another seven sleepless nights struggling to recapture something long forgotten, as the first early morning lights filtered into the bedroom, Eleanor was suddenly aware that she was coming into the memory.

Her hand suddenly went up to her forehead. That's it, she thought. We bumped heads really hard. He had dropped something and I helped him pick it up. What was it? It was right after he opened the investment firm.

She finally fell into an uneasy sleep and began to dream — fragments that came and went. She was in the office. We bumped heads. He was nervous.

With that, Eleanor's memory faded. She had heard somewhere that if you write a dream down, it will help you to remember it clearly. And if you put your mind on a search-and-retrieve pattern, you may find what you're looking for.

Suddenly hopeful, Eleanor got out of bed quietly so as not to awaken Frank, slipped on her robe, and went out to the kitchen.

She got the pad that she used to jot her grocery list and took a pen from the drawer.

Sitting at the kitchen table, she began to write. "Mr. Bennett and I bumped heads . . . It was just after I started working for him." She hesitated. "He dropped something because he had just come in. It was very cold out. He said his fingers were stiff. He was terribly nervous."

There was nothing more that she could bring back yet.

33

Sylvie de la Marco was in an increasingly bad mood. She knew she had to call Parker for more money soon. Two million more, just for the decorating!

And she had gone through a lot of money, a whole lot of money, last year. She'd bought a lot of clothes, which she absolutely needed because she was out socially so much.

And she had gone to Brazil last year. The surgery there was superb. She knew she didn't look more than thirty, which was just right for someone who was actually forty-six.

What was the matter with Parker? He had stolen five billion dollars. Why was he being so miserly?

She realized she had begun to worry. Was it possible that after accumulating all that money, Parker had lost some or most of it?

And what happened if they ever *caught*

him? It would be just like him to turn her in.

These were Sylvie's troubled thoughts as, in a new Chanel suit, her Russian sable coat slung over her arms, she was almost ready to leave to have lunch with an A-list friend, Pamela Winslow, at Le Cirque.

Like her, Pamela had come from immigrant parents, hardworking, good people — Sylvie's Italian, hers Polish. Her parents named her Pansy because her mother loved *Gone with the Wind,* and she read that Scarlett's name was originally going to be Pansy. They giggled together about how they had begun planning to climb the social ladder to find a rich husband. They were both blessed with good looks. Pamela got her blond hair and blue eyes from her Polish ancestry. Sylvie helped hers along by dying her hair blond. It's always looked good with my brown eyes, Sylvie mused. Pamela and I were also both divorced twice.

Then Pansy landed a rich guy the year I married Eduardo, Sylvie thought. Now she has loads of money and I have to eke out a living begging droppings from Parker. But at least I have a title, and that really impresses people, most of the time.

It's time to look around, she thought.

As she headed for the front door, Robert

told her that Ms. Harper was in the drawing room. She had not specifically asked to see the countess.

She knows enough not to bother me, Sylvie thought, but decided that anyhow she would see what Harper was up to.

Glady had banished the heavy draperies and almost all of the furniture. "I know an upscale store where they sell secondhand household furniture and tchotchkes and get pretty decent prices for them," she had told Sylvie.

Now the drawing room was bare but painted in a soft vanilla shade that was a stark contrast to the harsh gold color that had been formerly there. Glady Harper was standing behind the painter as he began to paint the wainscoting.

"Ms. Harper," Sylvie said, her tone formal.

Glady turned. "Oh, good morning, Countess, or is it good afternoon?" She looked at her watch. "Oh, I guess either will do. It's about thirty seconds before noon."

As usual Sylvie was not sure if there was an underlying note of contempt in Harper's pleasant-enough greeting. She decided to ignore it. In the past month she had begun to realize that the whole feeling of the apartment was changing. Elegant but inviting was the way Harper had promised her it was going to be.

"Oh, Countess, before you go out, may I have a word with you?" Glady asked.

She's going to want more money, Sylvie thought, panicked. "Of course, Ms. Harper."

Glady walked toward her, then said, "I think we should step outside."

She must think that the painter can hear a bird pass wind, Sylvie thought as she stepped into the hallway.

Glady did not waste a minute. "The second installment is due next week," she said.

"Next week!"

"Of course, Countess. The paintings from Sotheby's; the salon furniture; the dining room table, chairs, sideboard, and chandelier; and the antique carpets throughout the house, as well as the fabric for the window treatments, all of which you approved, will be delivered within the next two weeks."

"Of course." Sylvie tried to sound assured, then added, "I don't think you gave me a schedule for the rest of the payments."

"I believe our contract specifically states the steps at which payments are due."

"Of course. You will have the check next week, Ms. Harper."

Remembering to keep her head up, Sylvie exited the apartment. She knew Robert would be in front with the car to drive her to Le Cirque. There certainly was no way that she would climb out of a cab in front of the doorman.

Pamela was already there. It was one of her little tricks to always be early for an appointment and make people feel as though they had kept her waiting.

Their date was for 12:30. It was just 12:20. "Hi, Pansy," Sylvie said just loud enough for the maître d' to hear.

"Hi, Sally."

They both laughed.

Over a gin martini they exchanged gossip. Sylvie knew that Pamela thought she was in touch with Parker, although she had never admitted to her that she was.

"How's Malcolm?" she asked.

"As rich as ever," Pamela replied. "And in equal parts, as boring."

Malcolm Winslow was a Wall Street investor, twenty-six years older than Pamela, his second wife. His shrewd tradings had made him a legend on Wall Street but his innate disdain for social events was a big problem for Pamela, who loved to see her picture in the paper.

Now, with a sigh, she asked, "What's new

with you, Sylvie?"

"The latest is that I'm redoing the apartment. Glady Harper is the decorator. She's a witch, but she is good."

Pamela raised her eyebrows. "And expensive, very, very expensive. And that is one big apartment. Twelve rooms, isn't it?"

Unfortunately, Sylvie remembered that Pamela was one of the few people who knew that she had received comparatively little from the de la Marco estate.

"Oh, I'm doing the whole thing. I might as well get it all over with. I guess I'll have to cast around for a rich husband."

"I think you should. Of course that means you'll have to trade off your title."

"Never. When I find that guy I won't take his name."

Over a salad and their second gin martini, Pamela turned serious. "Sylvie, I wasn't going to tell you this because I didn't want to upset you, but ever since Parker Bennett's secretary was indicted, the FBI has begun a new round of questioning people who were close to him. And they're telling people that there is a two-million-dollar reward for information leading to his conviction."

"Did they contact you?" Sylvie swallowed nervously.

"Yes."

"And what did you tell them?"

"What would you expect? I said that yes, you and I are good friends. I said I do not believe that you and Parker were involved personally, that the fact you were seen at dinner alone with Parker meant nothing. I said that you are a very good business-woman, that the count had dementia, and that you had a large investment in Parker's firm."

She paused. "How's that for a pal? But seriously, Sylvie, I think the interior decorating now might be a big mistake." Pamela took the last sip of her martini. "You know something you should consider? Barclay Cameron has always had an eye out for you. He told me so at La Grenouille last week. He said he's called you a couple of times, but you're always busy."

"Barclay Cameron! He's older than Eduardo."

"No he isn't. He's eighty-two, healthy, lonely, and a widower. Sylvie, my guess is that right now the Feds are going over your finances with a fine-tooth comb. If they can prove that you've been receiving big bucks from Parker Bennett, you could get twenty years in prison. That's what the FBI told me. I have a feeling they wanted me to pass that information on to you."

When the check came, they carefully split the bill.

34

The decorative pillows for Anne Bennett's living room arrived one week before Thanksgiving.

In the past two weeks, Lane had not heard from Eric. I understand why he hasn't called, she told herself. Eric must have been terribly upset about the picture in the gossip columns of the two of them.

That was what Anne Bennett told her the minute she arrived in Montclair.

"Oh, Lane. Eric has been so distressed about that picture," were her first words after she greeted Lane.

"Oh, he really shouldn't have been," Lane protested as she carried in a large plastic bag containing the pillows.

She took off her coat, dropped it on a chair in the foyer, and headed straight to the living room. One by one she took out the pillows and placed them on the couch and chairs, then stood back. "Just what I wanted," she told Anne. "It gives this room the oomph it needed."

As she spoke, Lane thought of Glady's burst of generosity. At the last minute Glady had decreed that the room's furnishings should not remind Anne of the fact that they had been used for the servants. "It's very pretty now," she had told Lane, "but that doesn't mean it can't be just as attractive with a different color scheme."

The couch was now in a sand shade, the chairs in a small floral pattern with a sand background.

Glady had chosen a Persian rug in red with a striking geometric pattern from one of the guest rooms that gave warmth and color to the room. "I know why the auctioneer didn't grab this," she had told Lane. "Without speaking to me, the Bennetts hired some idiot who cut off the original fringe and replaced it with glaring white cording." Glady later had had that fringe replaced by one that had an antique effect.

Anne had been surveying the room with delight. "Oh, Lane, you just don't know how much I love this place. I always felt like I was tiptoeing around the house for fear I'd break something."

It was eleven o'clock. "Lane, you've got to

have a cup of coffee with me," Anne said firmly.

There won't be any chance that Eric will show up for lunch this early, Lane thought. "I'd love a cup of coffee," she said sincerely.

She had had lunch in this kitchen a few weeks ago, but why did it feel as if she had been here many times? Lane asked herself. And why, even though she was sure Eric would not show up, did she find herself listening for the door to open and let her know that he was there?

Anne Bennett looks so much better and more animated, she thought as Anne placed the cup of steaming coffee in front of her and poured one for herself.

She sat down opposite Lane and smiled. "I have to tell you how pretty you are," she said. "And certainly Eric has said that to me one hundred times since he met you. Lane, I'm about to be sixty-seven years old and I've always been somewhat timid. From modest circumstances, Parker fit in with people who were rich and socially prominent from impeccable backgrounds. I never felt comfortable with those people. I always felt as though I was in a world where I didn't belong. I feel that I *belong* in this house and that through church I will get to make friends on my own."

She looked away for a moment. When she looked back at Lane, her eyes were glistening. "What I have to say is my great concern is my son. These past two years have been absolute hell for him. He lost many of his own accounts. He's pointed at wherever he goes. He couldn't have a dinner with you without being secretly photographed."

She took another sip of coffee, as though she was trying to compose herself. But then her eyes filled with tears. "Lane, Eric is very much in love with you. He told me that he cut that picture out of the newspaper and framed it for his apartment."

Lane didn't know what to say.

Anne sighed. "Remember that story about John Alden? He went to Priscilla to plead the case for her hand for his friend Captain Smith. Do you remember what Priscilla said?"

"She said something like, 'Why don't you speak for yourself, John?' " Lane answered.

"That's right, and despite what Priscilla advised, I'm pleading for Eric. You surely know the consequences of being seen in public regularly with him. But is there a chance that you can face that problem? Eric won't ask you to do that, but I can. Think it over."

Anne put down the cup and said, "Lane,

you don't have to respond now." She reached into her pocket and pulled out a small folded sheet of paper. She passed it across the table to Lane. "You probably have it already but here is Eric's cell phone number. If he doesn't hear from you, he will understand and never contact you again. And I guess you've finished the last of the decorating, haven't you?"

"Yes, we have," Lane said quietly.

"Well then, this may be good-bye but I hope and pray it is not."

Five minutes later, Lane was driving back to New York.

I don't know what to do, she thought.

I simply don't know what to do.

35

There was one kind of crook Joel Weber despised over any other. That was the one who in some way caused injury to a child. In his long career he had dealt with a number of cases where someone deliberately murdered a child and tried to get rid of the body. It had been his savage pleasure to help convict them through the evidence he uncovered.

Next on his list was a sophisticated thief who preyed on decent hardworking people who were diligently putting aside money for their retirement or to pay for their children's college expenses.

These were the little people who were sweet-talked by crooks like Bennett and ended up with nothing but the roof over their heads, if they were lucky. Sometimes not even that. A number of Parker Bennett's victims had taken mortgages on their homes because of his advice. Make your money make money for you — that was Parker Bennett's pitch.

It was mathematically impossible for Parker to have done all the necessary paperwork alone. He had to have had at least one, if not two, people in on the scheme with him.

Joel had considered Bennett's wife, Anne, as a possible co-conspirator. She and Bennett had worked in the same investment firm before he went out on his own. But she had retired after their marriage forty-five years ago. When the fraud was discovered, she had been thoroughly investigated but nothing came of it. In the few years she had worked at the trading firm, she had been a secretary, pure and simple. Her job had been to take dictation, type letters, and answer the phones.

In the years leading up to when the Bennett Fund failed and he disappeared, she hadn't owned a computer. All the servants in Greenwich attested to that.

Her son, of course, was a different story. At twenty-two he had started his career in compliance at Morgan Stanley. That gave him technical training and access to that firm's computer database of statements, which he could have funneled to his father. Then Parker could have changed the names and some figures on the statements, put them on his firm's letterhead, and sent them out to his investors.

Joel had made a list of all the schools Eric Bennett had attended. They were the usual ones to be expected for a rich child with an excellent brain: Greenwich Country Day School through eighth grade, Andover Prep in Westfield, Connecticut, and Magna Carta College in Montpelier.

In the middle of his first semester of his sophomore year at Magna Carta, Eric had withdrawn and switched to Trinity College in Dublin. He had graduated from there.

I can see why he might have wanted a year abroad, Joel thought, *but why switch schools so suddenly? Did something go wrong at that point? Did he get in any kind of trouble? Was he staying out of the country for any reason?*

I'll start there and see what I can find out, he decided.

The next day he drove up to Montpelier, Vermont, and went into the office of student affairs at Magna Carta. There he was politely told that records showed that Eric Bennett had withdrawn on his own and there was no further information they could give him.

Dissatisfied, Joel walked over to the school library. On a hunch he looked up the list of benefactors to the school.

And found what he wanted. The same month Eric Bennett had abruptly left, his father, Parker Bennett, had made a ten-million-dollar donation to the college development fund.

36

Parker Bennett began to make his final preparations for leaving St. Thomas. Two years ago he had disappeared from his life as Parker Bennett with nothing but the clothes on his back.

Sometimes he wondered what had happened to the custom suits and jackets and ties and shirts and shoes in his closets in Greenwich. Did they sell or donate them? He hoped Anne wasn't sentimental enough to keep them and let them rot in the closet. His mother had done that when his father died. Good God, Parker thought. We had two clothes closets in that dreary apartment and one of them was a shrine to that guy. Dropped dead of a heart attack after finishing his rounds as a postman. Only forty-seven years old, but a smoker. Every picture of him showed him holding a butt.

This time Parker was going to be sure that the clothes he bought were as nondescript as possible. Zip-up winter jacket, cap with earmuffs, heavy shoes.

He still couldn't be sure if he would make a date to meet Sylvie. He wasn't sure if he could trust her. He knew he had made a mistake showing her how upset he was when she asked him for two million dollars last week. The last thing he wanted was for her to think he was short of money. The next time she called he'd be much nicer and say, "Of course, dear, right away."

There was something else. He had read in the business section of the *Wall Street Journal* that the FBI was offering a two-million-dollar reward for information that would lead to his capture.

That was a new wrinkle. That kind of reward wasn't usually made public in cases like this. Was there any chance that Sylvie had let something slip? Maybe to one of her friends after a few gin martinis? That possibility had always been lurking in the background of his mind, but now, with the announcement of the reward, it had become a full-fledged threat.

He had told people around here that he would be leaving in the next six weeks because of his job with the English government. He didn't want to give them the sense that he was in any kind of hurry.

It wouldn't be suspicious to say that the timing had been moved up and that he was leaving at the end of the month.

He had a golf date with Len this afternoon. He had to make it. Then if Len did talk about his resemblance to Parker Bennett, he'd remind him of that guy who looked so much like Lyndon Johnson that he posed for a whiskey ad and was paid to walk on the set of the Johnny Carson show and pass in back of Johnny without saying a word. This was when Johnson was in the White House.

Then he could always joke about the poem most people his age had read when they were in high school. It was about twins who looked alike. The last line was "And when I died they buried my brother John."

That should do it, Parker thought as he felt himself rebuilding his confidence in his ability to throw that self-styled joker off course.

And today he would regretfully tell him that he would be leaving soon to go back to England.

37

Agent Jon Pierce, alias Tony Russo, had installed an eavesdropping system so sophisticated that even a sweep of Anne Bennett's town house would not have detected it.

He had done it the second Sunday when he saw Anne leave for Mass, the day he spotted the old black car driving past the town house. It had been easy to get into the house undetected. The security system sensor was on the door leading from the garage into the den. Of course there was another one at the front door but there was no way he would take the chance on someone seeing him going in there.

It had not taken him much time to bug the interior. When Anne Bennett arrived home, she did not know that every word she said in the living room, kitchen, dining room, bedrooms, and den would be recorded.

That first Sunday he had heard nothing that was of any use. Anne Bennett was not someone who talked to herself. She was on the telephone only once and there was nothing in her conversation to a friend that had any meaning for him.

His job was to see if either Anne or her son was in touch with Parker Bennett.

Jon knew Eric's New York apartment was bugged, and Eric would be too smart to say anything incriminating over any phone that might be tapped. But he *did* visit his mother every other evening to have dinner with her. He had come to dinner last Sunday night.

Anne brought up Parker Bennett's name. She had said, "Eric, I know you'll think I'm crazy, but something in me is telling me that your father is still alive."

Eric's answer had been, "Mom, try to put that thought out of your mind. And if he is, can you imagine how awful it would be for Dad to spend the rest of his life in prison? Because that's what will happen if he is found."

Anne Bennett's answer had been, "Eric, suppose if your father is alive and they find him and he still has most of the money. Wouldn't they give him a break? I mean, couldn't he say that he had a mental breakdown?"

"Mom, nobody is going to give him a break and nobody is going to care about any mental breakdowns. There's a two-million-dollar reward for anyone who can tell the FBI where to find Dad. If he is alive, I assure you that anyone who knows where he is will be rushing to get that reward."

Anne's next question shocked Jonathan Pierce. "How about that girlfriend of his, the countess? If your father is alive, I'll bet he's in touch with her."

"Mom, Dad never thought you knew about her."

As Jonathan listened, he realized that Anne Bennett had a totally honest core of reality, and that she was challenging her son.

"Eric," she said. "I believe you are innocent of your father's crime. I'm still not sure whether or not you are in touch with him if he's alive. I certainly am not deaf, dumb, or blind. I always realized, even when I married him, that Parker was the kind of man who would probably stray."

There was a pause as Jonathan strained to hear, trying not to miss a word of the conversation.

"Eric," Anne Bennett continued, "I've been aware of all your father's affairs. But the way I've looked at it is that there are marriages where the wife can exist happily knowing the kind of man she married and is capable of living with it in a nontraditional way. Your father was involved with the countess for about eight years, and with many other women before that, in the years before he disappeared. But if he is still alive and she knows it, I'm afraid for him. If she finds out there is a reward, she would be just the kind to turn him in, if she knows where he is."

Eric left soon after and for a long time Jonathan sat quietly absorbing what he had heard.

Anne Bennett was clearly warning Eric that if his father was still alive, Countess Sylvie de la Marco might be a threat to him, and that he should give him that message.

Later that week he listened as a tearful Anne Bennett pleaded with Lane to understand how much Eric was in love with her.

This from a woman who suspects that her husband is still alive and her son is in touch with him!

Don't get caught up in this mess, Lane, he thought. Don't get caught up in it.

38

Timidly, but with a sense of excitement, Eleanor Becker dialed Sean Cunningham. He was at his desk. The writing of his book was going well and Sean almost decided to ignore the call and let the answering machine take a message. But when he saw on the ID that it was Eleanor Becker, he rushed to pick it up.

"Eleanor," he said. "How are you, and how's Frank?"

"I'm what you'd expect and Frank, well, you know, Sean, all this tension is not good for him."

"Of course it isn't."

"Sean, remember you told me that there may have been a few times when something hit me as odd, I mean about Parker Bennett?"

"Yes I do." Let there be something of substance, Sean prayed.

"Well, you see, I've been really trying to

search my memory. And the other night I came up with something."

As Sean listened, Eleanor explained about bumping heads with Parker Bennett. "I mean it wasn't just a little bump. Now I remember he had dropped some cards out of his wallet, and when I reached for one of them, he lunged at it. I think now that he was afraid to have me see it."

"Eleanor, when did this happen?"

"It was when we moved into the new office."

That was the beginning of the fraud, Sean thought. "Eleanor, do you know what kind of card that was?"

"It's come back to me. It was a driver's license, but not an American one. I just can't remember anything more than that, even though I think I did get a pretty good look at it."

"Eleanor, this could be very important. Would you consider being hypnotized to see if we can learn more about what information may be on that card?"

"That's a little scary. Does it hurt?"

"No, Eleanor. There is absolutely no pain attached to hypnosis."

"I mean, I'm not afraid of pain. It's just such a strange idea to me. But if it helps to find Mr. Bennett, or where the money is,

209

I'd be glad to do it."

"Eleanor, this could be nothing, but it may be worth everything to try it. I'll make an appointment with a psychiatrist who is also a very good hypnotist and I'll get back to you."

Sean did not put down his cell phone after he said good-bye to Eleanor. Instead he immediately dialed Rudy Schell and told him what was going on.

"Rudy, I've heard that in some cases the FBI uses hypnosis to help people recall certain events?"

"Yes we do, Sean. Why are you asking?"

"Because it's possible that Eleanor Becker needs to fully recall something that happened right at the beginning of Parker Bennett's fraud. She thinks she saw a driver's license that definitely was not an American one, and that Parker rushed to get it out of her hand."

Rudy had hoped that the publicizing of a two-million-dollar reward might be a lure for anyone who had any shred of evidence to offer, but Sal Caparo, the agent who made the rounds of people who had been seen frequently with Bennett, had drawn a blank.

His biggest hope had been Pamela Winslow, a close friend of Countess Sylvie de la Marco. The fact that they knew each other in Staten Island and had remained close friends made Rudy hope that the countess might have confided something about Parker to her.

But of course to someone married to a billionaire, the two-million-dollar reward was pocket change. Pamela had vigorously defended her friend, even to the point of saying that Sylvie de la Marco only saw Parker on a business basis.

But now, maybe, Eleanor Becker could provide meaningful evidence under hypnosis that would help them apprehend Parker Bennett at last.

39

Ranger figured out where to buy a gun, but he didn't have any idea about what kind of gun he should buy. He drove his car into one of the housing developments in the Bronx that was known to be a high-crime area.

This time his car fit well in the rundown neighborhood with its broken windows, trash-filled streets, and permeating sense of desolation.

He drove cautiously, noting with concern the young men hanging out in groups of three or four on the street corners. He wasn't really sure what he should do. Do I go up to one of those guys? he asked himself. Suppose they don't have a gun? Suppose they're okay kids and turn me in to the cops?

Moistening his dry lips with his tongue, he slowly cruised the neighborhood. Then he stopped at a traffic light and a kid who didn't look more than sixteen sidled up to the car and tapped on the window.

"Hey dude. What are you looking for?" he asked. "Pot, smack, coke?"

Ranger swallowed hard, unable to speak for a moment. Then, his voice hoarse, he whispered, "There's a guy out to get me. I need a gun."

"Sure, what kind?"

"I don't know — something simple. I mean, I only want it for protection."

"Sure you do. Ever use a gun?"

"No."

"All right. Let's make it easy for you. Man, you want a Smith and Wesson .38 Special. Pull over to the curb."

Ranger parked as the kid disappeared down the alleyway between two apartment buildings. In five minutes he was back, his right hand in his pocket. He glanced up and down the street, obviously looking for a police car, and then pulled his clenched right hand from his pocket. "The best," he said proudly. "Like I promised, a .38 Special Smith and Wesson, two-inch barrel, easy to use. Loaded. You got five shots before you have to reload it." He handed it to Ranger.

Ranger held the gun gingerly but liked the feel of it. "You said five shots?"

"Five. The cops had this kind of gun for a

time. No harder than using a water pistol."
The kid laughed. "But whoever gets hit with
it at close range won't think he got hit by
no water pistol. Most likely he'll be dead."

Nervously, Ranger put the gun in the
glove compartment.

"How much?" he asked.

"Two hundred bucks."

Ranger wanted nothing more than to get
away, out of this neighborhood where a cop
would be sure something was going on, seeing him parked here and the kid leaning in
the window. He pulled out his wallet. He
handed the money to the kid.

As he was closing the window and starting the car he was unaware of the kid's
friendly, "Anytime, dude."

Nor was he aware that the kid burst out
laughing when he counted the money. Two
hundreds bucks for an old pistol, he
thought, and then the dope was so nervous
he gave me an extra twenty by mistake.
Can't have a better day than this!

40

The Monday after Lane's visit to Anne Bennett, Lane and Glady were at the countess's apartment awaiting the arrival of two antique Bashir rugs for the salon.

"Do you remember what La-di-da said when I showed her pictures of them?" Glady asked Lane.

"Sure I do. She thought they looked a little dull. She says she likes bright colors."

The rugs had a soft pallette of creams, beiges, and terra-cotta that would project old-world elegance within a more modern context. The ceiling and paneling of the salon were now creamy beige. Austrian crystal chandeliers were hanging above the two seating areas.

"I hope she gets smart enough to appreciate all this," Glady said tartly.

Then, switching subjects as usual, she asked, "Lane, what's the matter with you? You look as though you just lost your best friend. It depresses me to see that long face on you. What's going on?"

Lane was not sure whether she wanted to confide in Glady but then decided to go ahead. "When I brought out those pillows to Anne Bennett's apartment . . ."

"The ones I gave her for free?"

"I know, Glady. The gist of it is that Anne told me that Eric cares very deeply for me and that he has been afraid to call me because I might have been upset about our picture together being in the *Post.*"

"As he should be," Glady snapped.

"Glady, I believe Eric is innocent."

"I don't."

"I know that, but hear me out. I'm certainly not ready for a serious relationship with Eric, but I do like him and don't want to be one of the people who would reject him because of his father. In fact I'm going to call him. The problem is that Katie was getting so attached to him."

"Lane, if you're going to keep seeing this guy in any way, do yourself a favor. Don't meet him at your apartment, because it's obvious he would see Katie there. Whenever possible don't go to a restaurant in Manhattan. Now that you've been seen with him the paparazzi may not be interested, but there are plenty of people out there who feed gossip to the columnists."

She stopped. "There's the doorbell. The rugs are probably here."

As two burly deliverymen unrolled them, Glady picked up where she'd left off. "Lane, my final word on the subject is you should go to New Jersey and meet him at some restaurant there. Have dinner with him, then drive yourself home. There's a two-million-dollar reward for information leading to the arrest of his father that's just become public. I wouldn't be surprised if somebody who knows something, like her Royal Nobody here, may start singing. And if they catch Parker Bennett and he decides to tell all, I'll bet every nickel I ever made in my life that it will come out that Eric and Parker's fingers were in the same cookie jar."

That evening, after Katie was in bed, Lane called Eric. He answered on the first ring. "Lane, how are you?"

"I'm good." She hesitated. "You must know that your mother talked to me about us?"

"Yes. Is this a brush-off?"

"No, it isn't, Eric. I enjoy being with you and I'd like to see you, but I'm not ready to go any further than to have dinner every week or so, at least for a while."

"It's as much as I can hope for. Lane, I only wish they'd catch my father if he is still alive. That's the only way my name will ever be cleared. When can we meet?"

"I'm going to my mother's in Washington with Katie for Thanksgiving. I'll be back on Sunday." She was not sure what Eric might say. He certainly was aware of what her stepfather, Dwight Crowley, had been writing about him.

But there was no change in the tone of his voice as he said, "You'll be back on Sunday. I'll call you Sunday evening. Happy Thanksgiving to you and Katie, Lane."

Before she could answer, Eric ended the call.

41

On the day before Thanksgiving, a distinctly nervous Eleanor Becker met Sean Cunningham at the office of Dr. Steven Papetti, who was both a psychiatrist and a hypnotist in Manhattan.

Sean had asked Eleanor if she would permit Rudy Schell to be present during the session. "Eleanor, I know he is sympathetic to you and he very much hopes that the hypnosis causes you to remember information that will help them find Bennett. This can only help you on your own case. Talk to your lawyer and see if it's okay with him."

"I will call him and just tell him I'm going to do it," Eleanor replied firmly. "I don't care what he says and I'm not paying him to sit there and watch. And I agree with you, Sean. Deep down, I think that Rudy Schell believes that I am innocent."

When he saw her, Rudy sprang from his

chair and hurried over to Eleanor. Under his shock of gray-streaked black hair, the expression on his ruddy face was concerned, and he took her hand in both of his.

"Mrs. Becker," he said in a gentle voice. "I understand why you feel you have every reason to consider me hostile to you. But please let me reassure you. It is my job as an agent in the Federal Bureau of Investigation to find evidence and build a case against criminals. It is also our sacred obligation to protect innocent people from wrongful punishment. You have always maintained that you had no involvement in Parker Bennett's theft."

"None whatsoever," Eleanor said, her voice breaking. "I feel so sorry for every one of those poor people who lost their money. I guess I'm stupid, terribly, terribly stupid, but I thought he was not only a businessman but a philanthropist."

Frank put a protective arm around his wife. "It's okay, honey, it's okay." He looked at Rudy. "Are you on the level that you can keep an open mind about Eleanor's involvement in this mess?"

"Absolutely," Rudy answered promptly.

Sean was standing back, ready to greet them. "Eleanor," he said. "You're doing a great job. You've started to remember the incident that seemed odd to you. Now with Dr. Papetti's help you may remember most of it or all of it. Do you remember that old commercial about Ivory Soap?"

"Ninety-nine and forty-four one hundredths pure," Eleanor said smiling. "But I used Camay, 'the soap for beautiful women.' I thought if I used it, I'd be beautiful too."

"You are a Camay beauty, and with a little luck your memory will be as pure as Ivory Soap."

As they both laughed, Rudy, watching them, observed how fragile both Eleanor and Frank Becker had become.

In the past two years, they had not only both lost weight, but their expressions were alike — despondent and wary, as if waiting for another blow. But that sudden touch of humor from Eleanor reminded him once again of what happens to people who get caught up in the justice system. Anyone he had interviewed about Eleanor at the beginning of the investigation had described her as having a good sense of humor. This was the first time he had ever seen a touch of it.

They had barely hung up their coats when the woman at the reception desk invited them to follow her into the doctor's office.

Dr. Steven Papetti was a handsome man

221

in his midfifties or so, with a thick head of graying hair. He stood up from his desk as they came in and greeted them with a friendly smile. Clutching Frank's hand, Eleanor nodded timidly to him.

The room was large. A La-Z-Boy leather chair was a few feet from the window that faced into the room. Across from it was a standard office chair, the kind that swiveled. There were also three folding chairs set halfway between the La-Z-Boy and the desk.

Dr. Papetti invited Eleanor to sit down and lean back in the La-Z-Boy chair.

"I imagine you don't quite know what to expect?" His voice was gentle.

"No, I guess I do, but no, I don't really."

"Well, let's talk about why you're here, Eleanor."

"Well, I guess you know that I'm here because I'm trying to remember something that may help the police find Parker Bennett, the man who swindled so many people of their life savings."

"That's exactly right, Eleanor. Dr. Cunningham has probably told you that going under hypnosis is absolutely painless. What we are trying to do is go down into your memory and try to retrieve the information you may have. It's not unlike looking for something you misplaced, like

222

keys or a cell phone."

Eleanor smiled. "Oh, I know all about that. It seems to me that never a day goes by without me looking for my glasses, and it feels pretty good when you find them."

It was obvious to Sean that Eleanor was becoming relaxed under Dr. Papetti's gentle approach.

"Eleanor, you know that Dr. Cunningham and Agent Rudy Schell will be here while you and I are working."

"And Frank," she quickly added. For a moment her voice was fearful. "Frank is going to stay, isn't he?"

"Of course he is. Eleanor, why don't you lean back in the chair until your feet are up? You don't have to go all the way back. You can be quite comfortable in a slightly reclined position. And now I want you to close your eyes and forget that any of us are here."

"I'll try."

Sean, Rudy, and Frank listened intently as Dr. Papetti, his voice quiet and soothing, invited Eleanor to imagine getting into an elevator. The elevator would stop at every one of ten floors and she would enjoy the ascent.

"Are you comfortable with that idea?" he asked Eleanor.

"I guess so. It's fine." She looked appealingly at Frank. When he gave her a thumbs-up, she leaned back.

"Eleanor," Dr. Papetti began, "close your eyes and think about getting into the elevator." Slowly, slowly, he took her up, stopping at every floor of a ten-story building. Then he said, "Eleanor, we're going to start going down in the elevator. You are sinking deeper and deeper as the elevator descends. Are you enjoying the trip?"

"Yes." Eleanor's voice had taken on a monotone quality.

"Ninth floor, eighth floor, seventh floor." Dr. Papetti continued to ask her if she knew she was going down.

Finally, when the imaginary elevator reached the first floor, Dr. Papetti said, "Eleanor, I think it's time for you to go back into Parker Bennett's office. You have only recently begun to work for him. Tell me about the office."

In a halting voice, Eleanor began to speak. "It's such a pretty office."

"How big is it, Eleanor?"

"It has a reception area, and Mr. Bennett has a big private office."

"How is it furnished?" Papetti asked.

"He fixed it up so it's very comfortable. It has a little kitchen off of it. That's where I

224

make tea or coffee for people who come to see Mr. Bennett."

"Do you have your own office, Eleanor?"

"Oh yes. It's down the hall. It's where I keep my paperwork, copies of letters I write inviting people to meet Mr. Bennett. Usually, I sit at the reception desk answering the phone and greeting people when they come in."

"Does anyone else work there, Eleanor?"

"No, not in the office. The paperwork for client accounts is handled by people at other locations."

"Do you like Mr. Bennett, Eleanor?"

"Oh, you couldn't meet a nicer man." Her voice lost some of its lack of expression. "But then suddenly one day he wasn't there, and then money was missing and people thought it was my fault too."

"Eleanor, do you remember the day you and Parker Bennett bumped heads?"

"Yes I do."

"Can you remember what happened?"

"Well, it was just at the beginning of when I went to work for him. It was very cold out that day. When he came into the office he took off his gloves and told me that he had waited for a cab outside the restaurant and his fingers were frozen. He took off his overcoat. His wallet was in the back pocket of his pants. I could see it sticking out from under his suit jacket." There was a long hesitation. Finally, she continued. "I said, 'Mr. Bennett, your wallet is about to fall out of your pocket. I hope you didn't lose anything.' He didn't say anything. He just grabbed the wallet and saw that the flap that held the credit cards was open and a couple of them were sticking up." Her voice hesitated.

"Eleanor, what did you see then?"

"I don't know."

"Eleanor, think of how nice it is to go down in the elevator, how warm it feels."

As the three men sat tensely, hoping, there was a long pause, then Eleanor began to speak again.

"His fingers were cold. All his cards fell out and were on the floor. He was nervous. His hands were shaking. We both bent down to pick them up but he told me not to bother. But I was already bending down and we bumped heads."

"What kind of cards did you see, Eleanor?"

"His driver's license, his credit cards . . . then I picked up a card."

"What card, Eleanor?"

"A driver's license. It was sort of pink and his picture was on it."

226

"His picture was on it?" Dr. Papetti asked quietly.

"Oh yes. His cousin's card . . . England."

"You saw his cousin's picture, Eleanor?"

"It looked like him. He said it was his cousin."

"Eleanor, did you see the name on the license?"

There was a long pause.

"Can't remember. Can't remember."

Another long pause.

"George. I know it's George."

It was not possible for Eleanor to remember any further details of that day. She was clearly waking up. The session was over.

When she was fully awake, she said again, "His first name was George."

"That's right, Eleanor," Dr. Papetti replied.

"But I couldn't remember his last name."

"Do you think you saw it on the license?" Papetti asked.

"Yes."

Eleanor started to get up. As Frank rushed to help her from the chair, Sean and Rudy looked at each other. Rudy spoke first.

"Well, we now know what we've suspected for some time. The fraud started the day he opened that office. He was establishing another identity for himself. Eleanor told us the picture was of his English cousin. I believe it was a picture of Bennett in disguise. I bet that license is British, which narrows down the search to England, and maybe some other parts of the Commonwealth."

Eleanor came over and began apologizing to everyone. She was crying again.

"If they don't find Mr. Bennett, I'll probably go to prison," she sobbed.

"Eleanor, your mind is working for you right now," Dr. Papetti said soothingly. "I want you to come back again next week. You *are* sure you saw the last name on that license?"

"Yes, I am. Very sure."

"Then maybe the next time you come you will be able to retrieve it from your memory." He patted her shoulder soothingly. "I can't promise you that you will remember, but I have seen it happen many, many times. Have faith."

42

After her lunch date with Pamela, Sylvie de la Marco had done considerable thinking. Her instinct told her that either Parker had somehow lost his money, or for some reason he couldn't get his hands on a lot of money anymore. There was no mistaking the decidedly serious tone in his voice. On the other hand, that nervousness might easily have been because he thought the Feds were closing in on him.

Suppose they *did* catch him? Wouldn't his first words be about her? For two years she had been pretty demanding.

Sylvie smiled. *Very* demanding. She had sometimes cut out ads from the *Times*. Tiffany almost always had an ad on page two for new jewelry. She described it to him and told him how much it cost. On the opposite side of the page Chanel advertised the dearest handbags, and she described them to him too. She had accounts with most of the haute couture designers, and she paid the bills with the money he wired to her.

And of course she was receiving a monthly allowance from both Parker and the de la Marco estate.

Parker had been generous until now, no doubt about that. He had also reminded her that if she ever considered turning him in, she would face twenty years in prison for aiding and abetting.

It's been good up till now, Sylvie thought as she made her daily visit to every room in the apartment. She did realize that Glady's interior design gave it a totally different look. Her friends who visited raved about it. One of them had gushed to *Architectural Digest* about how beautiful it was and they had made a date to do a photo spread when it was completed.

Sylvie grinned as she thought about that. She remembered that her mother had put flowered slipcovers on the living room furniture during the summer and changed the wool rug for a straw one. I really enjoyed those big flowers on the couch and chairs. So nice and bright, not understated elegance. Of course half the cost of the decorating now was in paintings and sculptures.

"What you are getting are the works of new and exciting painters and sculptors," Glady had told her crisply. "Every one of these will be worth at least triple in ten years. Look up what a Picasso cost when he was a struggling artist."

All well and good, Sylvie thought, but if Parker gets caught and turns me in, I go to prison too, and what good will they do me then? But there is a way out. I'll go to Derek Landry. Everybody knows he's the best lawyer for someone in my kind of situation. I'll tell him that Parker threatened me. If I ever didn't accept his gifts or stopped taking money, he would get a hit man and I'd be dead in twenty-four hours. I'll tell him that I must have anonymity guaranteed by the Feds or I'll never feel out of danger.

Meanwhile she was sure Barclay Cameron would call. Pamela had passed the word that she'd love to hear from him. To make sure she looked her best when they got together she had spent the morning at Salon Henri. Now her hair was newly blond, her skin glowing. She'd had a manicure and pedicure and her eyebrows had been threaded.

Yesterday she had bought a new Chanel suit, a winter-white shade. In other words, she was ready for Barclay's call.

It came at three o'clock. Robert answered,

of course, and hurried to tell her Mr. Barclay Cameron was calling. Trying not to grab the phone from him, Sylvie, in her most cultivated voice, said, "Barclay, how are you?"

"Sylvie, is it possible that you might be interested in dining with me?"

The well-bred voice had an excited note in it. Sylvie reminded herself that Barclay may be eighty-two but he had been interesting enough. She had had a brief fling with him, years ago, but then Parker came along and that was that with Barclay.

Parker — she had been in love with him and enjoyed their secret trysts for the last six years of Eduardo's life. But then Eduardo died and Parker disappeared, and what was she supposed to do?

"Yes, Barclay, I would love to dine with you. It's good to hear your voice."

"And it's good to hear yours. But I'd rather see and be with you."

Sylvie had forgotten that Barclay always thought he was witty with his little plays on words. But who cared about that?

"That's just what I'd like," she answered, a smile in her voice. He had been a recent widower when they met, and childless. She had been a fool to let him go. And he had never remarried.

"Are you free for dinner early next week, Sylvie? Does Tuesday work?"

"Wonderful. How about a cocktail here first?"

"I would enjoy that very much. See you then."

Sylvie replaced the receiver. It was definitely time to make a deal with the Feds, otherwise it might be too late.

She had met Derek Landry at a few big parties. She looked up his number, went into the library, and closed the door. She certainly wasn't going to risk being overheard by the servants.

Seconds later she was speaking to the famous lawyer.

"Derek, I have a little problem," she began.

43

The day before Thanksgiving Lane and Katie took the train to Washington.

Katie was thrilled to be seeing her grandmother. Lane had limited most of their visits to times when Dwight was away and she was uncomfortably aware that those visits were far too infrequent.

It had been August when she was last in Washington, and as usual Dwight had not been there.

But this year there was no refusing her mother's invitation. She had said, "Lane, let's get something clear. No more excuses about why you can't come home for Thanksgiving. If you're worried that Dwight will say one word about Eric Bennett, you can be assured that his lips are sealed. He knows how hard it is for me that you don't like him. It's about time you realized that. I loved your father dearly and I mourned him for ten years before I remarried. I'm very happy with Dwight, but very sad that you always avoid him."

All this was on Lane's mind on the three-hour ride down from Penn Station to Washington. Katie had read a few of her books and then fallen asleep, her head on Lane's lap. *How will I feel if, in thirteen years, when Katie is seventeen, she rejects me for some reason?*

Eric — Eric — Eric. She knew she should take it slowly but after three dates with him, Lane was very much looking forward to the next one.

Anne Bennett had been delighted to know that Eric and she were seeing each other. She had invited Katie and Lane to have Thanksgiving dinner with them at her town house.

"I'm having it catered," she said. "I never want to go out for dinner on holidays. And I'd love to meet your Katie."

It had been less awkward to say she was going to Washington to be with her mother than to outright refuse the invitation.

The train was slowing down. She had told her mother that it was easier for them to take a cab than for Alice to try to park near the station.

But there was another reason. She would have the driver pass the house they had lived in in Georgetown for the first seventeen years of her life. But it was the first seven years that she had been dreaming about lately.

It was always about her father. In the dream he was so vivid to her. The memories of sitting on his lap and reading together . . . the trips to the Smithsonian where he explained what they were seeing together . . . the times they went ice skating. He was a naturally good skater; she was just okay. The time when she was four years old and darted ahead of him into the street and was almost hit by a car. He had grabbed her by her sweater, yanked her back just in time. Then he had picked her up and hugged her so hard she could hardly breathe even while he sternly warned her to never, never do that again.

They walked through Union Station and easily got a cab, and Lane gave the driver the address. Twenty minutes later she felt tears sting her eyes as they turned down the street, which was only three blocks from Dwight's larger home. "Just slow down a bit past that house," she told the driver.

"Someone you know live there?" the driver asked.

Lane did not want Katie to talk about it to her mother. "Just a friend a long time ago." It looks the same, she thought. I feel as though I could open the door and walk in.

It was exactly five o'clock when the cab stopped at Dwight's home. It was built on a larger scale than the one where she had been raised and was an unmistakably impressive house.

Her mother was watching for them. She had the door open and was scooping up Katie before Lane had paid the driver. It was another reminder to Lane that Katie was missing something by not seeing more of her grandmother.

Alice put Katie down and turned to Lane slowly, as though afraid of rejection, then put her arms around her. Lane hugged her and planted a warm kiss on her cheek. "Hello, Mom. It's good to be here."

And it was.

"Dwight's fixing a cocktail for us. I told him that you liked chardonnay. Is that all right?"

"I could use one," Lane said, and then prayed that the words did not sound sarcastic.

They left their coats in the hall closet and Katie again ran ahead of them calling, "Poppa, Poppa," the name they had decided on for her to call Dwight.

The library was to the right of the foyer. The living room was down the hall. Dwight was at the bar there setting out glasses. Lane watched as he picked Katie up, gave her a peck on the cheek, lifted her onto a stool, and said, "At your service, ma'am. Shirley Temple, lemonade, or Sprite?"

"Shirley Temple," Katie answered promptly.

" 'Shirley Temple, please,' " Lane corrected.

As Katie dutifully repeated her request, adding "please," Lane and Dwight looked at each other. Lane knew that in his Harvard days Dwight had been editor of the school newspaper, the *Crimson,* and a star debater. Now his biting editorials in the *Washington Post* had earned both intense friends and equally intense enemies. Dwight was a very attractive man, she admitted to herself. He was about six feet tall with a disciplined body, a head of sandy gray hair, and dark hazel eyes.

She knew *about* him but she didn't know him, not really. She had never wanted to be close to him and now his ruthless comments about Eric had made it worse.

Their greetings to each other were tentative but his smile seemed to be genuine. "Lane, I'm so glad that you are able to make

238

it this year, and may I add that you're as pretty as your daughter."

Katie was sipping the Shirley Temple. "Mom tells me I'm beautiful," she said matter-of-factly.

Their shared laugh warmed up the temperature. Lane saw the relief on her mother's face and felt guilty.

The weekend went very well. Dwight's sister, Helen, and her husband, Gavin, came to dinner. They both worked on Capitol Hill. They seemed to enjoy Katie very much. Lane had seen little of them over the years and realized how truly interesting they were.

Helen clashed with her brother over politics several times during dinner. She told him, "Dwight, if you would only come down from your lofty peak and stop thinking you're an oracle of wisdom, you'd be better off. You might even see someone else's viewpoint."

Then, laughing, she had turned to Lane. "He really is a nice guy, he just finds it hard to show it."

On Saturday, Dwight suggested that they go to the Smithsonian and show Katie around.

Déjà vu all over again, Lane thought,

remembering the afternoons there with her father.

Over the weekend not a word about Eric Bennett passed Dwight's lips. A dozen times it was on the tip of Lane's tongue to ask him why he was so vehement about Eric, but she simply didn't want to risk getting into a confrontation with him.

On the way home on the train, Katie's reluctance to say good-bye to Nana and Poppa kept ringing in her ears. It was a guilty reminder that by keeping her away from Dwight, she had also been keeping her away from her mother.

"Mommy, you look sad," Katie commented.

"I'm not sad," Lane assured her. "I'm just thinking."

The fact that her mother and Dwight looked so happy and content together was a reminder of how terribly lonely she had been since Ken died. Of course she had dated in these five years, but no one had ever really interested her.

Until now. Anne Bennett had told her that Eric was in love with her. Could she allow herself to fall in love with him?

I don't know, she thought. I just don't know.

44

After discovering that Parker Bennett had made a ten-million-dollar donation to Magna Carta College at exactly the same time that Eric abruptly withdrew and transferred to Trinity College in Ireland, Joel Weber thought about what to do next. He looked up the students in the yearbook from the class that Eric would have graduated with had he stayed at Magna Carta. He wrote down the names of the students who had come from local areas and looked up their families' phone numbers. The first ten names yielded nothing. The numbers were either disconnected or had "leave a message" recordings. Probably half the parents, if they're still around, are in Florida, Joel thought, as he watched the snow falling outside his window.

On the tenth call Joel lucked out. A pleasant voice answered the call at the home of Carl Frazier.

Carefully, Joel explained his mission, skirting the truth without lying outright.

"I am with the Magna Carta College Library doing research. My name is Joel Weber. I am interested in speaking to students who went to Magna Carta at the time you were there."

"Then you want to be talking to my son. I am Carl Frazier Senior."

"Yes, I guess I do, sir," Joel said. "Can you tell me where to reach him?"

"He's a professor at Dartmouth College," his father responded.

"Can you give me his phone number?" Joel asked.

"Of course, just give me a moment."

A minute later Carl Frazier Sr. was back on the line.

"I have five kids," he explained. "They all have cell phones. I can't keep all their numbers straight. Here's Carl Jr.'s number. I know he will enjoy hearing from you. He loved his years at Magna Carta. It was a great experience for him."

It certainly wasn't a great experience for Eric Bennett, Joel thought as he wrote down the number.

When he dialed it, he listened to the usual annoying recording asking the caller to leave a message. What's so bad about putting your name on an answering device, he thought? At least that way you would be sure you had reached the right person.

Dartmouth College was only one hour away. He hoped that Professor Frazier wasn't away for the week. He decided to take a walk around the Magna Carta campus and look for the Bennett building. A student directed him to it. "Oh, they took the name off when it came out what a crook he was," the student explained. The building was in a row of student housing. Joel noticed with amusement that what must have been the Bennett name chiseled over the door was now covered in plaster, just as the student had said. Why did he give so much money when his son was on the way out the door? he wondered.

He remembered the fact that a college he had read about had received donations from three different high-powered executives, all of whom had gone to prison. The nickname of that lane on the college grounds was now "Felony Row." Not one of them was as bad as Bennett is, he thought. They did insider trading to enrich themselves, but they didn't steal the life savings of hundreds of people.

Restless, Joel decided to drive to Dartmouth's campus, rather than wait for Frazier's call.

I don't want to interview him by phone just to ask him about Eric Bennett. It might make him suspicious. I want to talk with him face-to-face, he thought as he got into his car and turned on the ignition.

It was an hour from Montpelier, Vermont, to Hanover, New Hampshire. The tranquil countryside was snow covered.

I went to a state college and got a good education but I wouldn't have minded being part of the Ivy League scene, Joel thought as he exited Route 89 and turned onto Route 91 North.

Dismissing that kind of foolishness, he was entering Hanover proper when his cell phone rang. He pressed the speaker button and said crisply, "Joel Weber."

It was Carl Frazier Jr.

Joel explained his reason for calling and requested a meeting. "I would like to ask you to give an impression of some of your classmates. Perhaps I can explain it better when I meet with you," Joel said.

"Sounds somewhat mysterious," was Carl Frazier's response. "Can you explain a little further now?"

"I will when we meet. I am only asking for half an hour of your time."

His voice somewhat cool, Frazier asked, "How close are you?"

"I just got off the highway and I'm crossing the river."

"Then let's meet at the Hanover Inn. I was about to drop in there for a cup of coffee."

Ten minutes later Joel was parking the car outside of the inn. It was not crowded and it was easy to pick out the man in his late thirties having coffee by the window.

Joel went over, greeted him, and without being invited, sat down.

When the waitress approached, he said, "Just coffee, please," and focused on the man across the table.

Frazier would be about Eric Bennett's age, he thought, thirty-seven. He looks a little older, but that's just because of his receding hairline. He wore rimless glasses and had a scholarly look about him. Even if he did not already know it, Joel would have guessed him to be an academic.

He decided to get right to the point. "When I called your father's home and got your number, I did not tell him that I'm with an investigative agency and I'm retired FBI."

Frazier raised his eyebrows. "I can't imagine what you would want with me," he said quietly.

"I simply want your impressions of a

classmate," Joel answered.

"And who would that be? No, let me guess, Eric Bennett?"

"That's exactly who I'm talking about," Joel replied.

"It wasn't hard to guess," Frazier explained to him. "Of course Eric was only at Magna Carta for one year, so none of us could say we even knew him well, but from what I remember, he was a nice enough guy."

"Why did he transfer so abruptly, at the beginning of his sophomore year?"

"Well, he got mugged pretty badly at that time. He was in the hospital for three days."

"Was it a random attack?" As Joel asked the question, he could sense that it had not been a random attack, not at all.

"Well, that was the strange part," Carl said. "As far as we all knew he never went to the police. He shrugged it off, even though he had a broken arm. Then his father made the donation, and he was off to Ireland."

"Do you think he left because he was afraid of being attacked again?" Joel persisted.

"Nobody really knows, although sometimes I wonder if someone on the faculty had an idea of what was up. The rumor was that Eric was asked to leave."

"Can you tell me the name of any student he was close to? Maybe a girlfriend?" Joel asked.

"There was one very pretty girl. She was in the local public high school. Eric brought her to the games. They seemed to spend a lot of time together," Carl said.

"She was in *high* school? How old would you think she was?"

"Sixteen," Carl responded.

Joel considered that a moment, then asked, "Was Eric ever into gambling as far as you know?"

"Well, he wasn't old enough to go to a casino, but he was very good at cards, and sometimes, for some of the guys with money, the stakes could get pretty high."

"Did anyone ever think that he was cheating?"

"I was in some of those games myself," Carl offered, "especially poker. Eric never had to cheat. He was a real card counter. He could make it in Vegas."

Nothing much here, Joel thought, except for the mugging, and for his getting out of town so fast. And then an idle question came to his head.

"Do you remember the high school girl's name?"

"Yes I do," Carl answered. "Regina Crowley. Her uncle is the political columnist Dwight Crowley."

After Frazier left, Joel used his iPhone to find the number of Montpelier High School. Google Maps showed that it was adjacent to the Magna Carta campus. The school secretary confirmed that the principal would be in all afternoon and would be available to meet with him. Fifteen minutes later Joel was back on the highway heading toward Montpelier.

45

Parker Bennett/George Hawkins was now counting the days until he could leave St. Thomas without appearing to be in any kind of rush. He had told whatever friends he had the story about going back to England at the end of the month. There was no way he wanted to change his plans so that there might be any suspicion about him. The seed had already been planted by Len Stacey's drawing attention to how much he looked like Parker Bennett. The brown wig and glasses were not a sufficient disguise if someone carefully studied his face. His only hope was that Len was too stupid to follow through and do any serious reflection on the similarity. He had had to stall on the last two million that Sylvie had demanded. When he sent that and the money for the villa in Switzerland, he would be down to his last five thousand dollars. And out of that money he would need to buy his plane ticket and pay to stay in Miami for at least three weeks until he could grow a beard, get a different wig, and go out to New Jersey and get into Anne's apartment.

Anne and Eric had always been close and Eric was certainly furious at him. Parker didn't know yet what he was going to do. Could he trust Anne not to turn him in? Would she, out of pity for the people who had lost their investments, be tempted to go the noble route? It had been easy to keep track of her these two years. Googling her had provided him with all the information he needed. And of course it was entirely possible she was still under surveillance. It certainly would be risky for him to just walk up to her door and ring the bell, but he may have no other choice. There were considerations that had to be planned for very, very carefully. He knew he was getting desperately nervous and that could be the source of his own undoing.

And of course there was Sylvie, always there was Sylvie. What would I do if I were in her boots? he wondered. I can only stall her for so long for the last two million. If she thinks I'm broke, I'm no good to her. More than that, she might try to make a deal with the FBI. They might give her a pass to get at me. He knew he had to get out of St. Thomas fast with the danger of Len's shooting off his mouth comparing George Hawkins with Parker Bennett. But in the meantime, he must not do anything unusual. He would golf a little and play at different public courses, go out on the boat every day, and hold his breath hoping that he wouldn't keep running into Len.

He made a list of the clothes he would buy for New Jersey — jeans, a heavy jacket, a hat with earmuffs, gloves, flannel shirts. All in dark colors of course. Nothing that would make anyone think about him twice. The fact that New Jersey was having a cold early winter would serve him well.

He would have to take several winter suits so that if he needed business attire, he would have it with him. He would not register anywhere as George Hawkins.

What would happen if Sylvie turned him in? If she did, George Hawkins was the man they would be looking for. It was not safe to use that name again. When he got to Miami, he would try to find out where fake ID's were sold. And then there was the matter of a passport. Could he get a new passport using his birth name Joseph Bennett while everyone was looking for Parker Bennett?

Thanksgiving day came and went. He had

a number of invitations and knew he could not use illness as an excuse again. Instead he said he already had plans. His housekeeper had cooked a small turkey for him. He thought of the Thanksgiving dinners in Greenwich with Anne and Eric. They seldom had guests for holiday dinners.

He knew that Anne was an uncomfortable and unwilling hostess, although she'd tried valiantly to appear at ease when he had had dinner parties with high-powered executives.

On Thanksgiving day she'd always insisted that it be just the three of them. Of course, that was after her parents died. Before that he had endured their presence regularly. He had been irritated that her father saw through his elaborate remake of himself. Every so often Anne's father would slip and call him Joey — a deliberate slip, of course. He always thought of Anne's father's hands as smelling slightly of liverwurst and bologna, a memory that amused him.

Anne's mother was exactly like Anne, ill at ease in the presence of anyone she considered her superior. Totally unlike Sylvie, who had vaulted herself out of her Italian grandmother's kitchen and its elaborate Sunday afternoon pasta meals attended by an obnoxious number of cousins and aunts and uncles. The minute she finished high school at age eighteen, she had put the whole bunch of them behind her for good.

All this Parker was thinking as he ate his solitary dinner, thoroughly contented with his own company.

The next day he began packing his suitcase. A few days more, he thought, and then I'm out of here. It was Friday. He managed to avoid Len for the next twenty-four hours, but then received a phone call on Saturday that dismayed him. The minute he heard, "Hi George," in that booming voice, he felt his palms begin to sweat and a knot form in the pit of his stomach.

"George, where have you been?" Len continued. "The guys were hoping to catch you this morning."

"Oh, I'm just enjoying the last few days on the boat. You know how I love to sail." He hoped his tone was sufficiently casual.

"Well, I have a surprise for you," Len said. "Dewayne and Bruce and I enjoyed playing golf with you so much that we decided we wanted you to join us on Monday. Let's have a final round of golf at nine o'clock and then we'll have lunch at the course. Don't say no, I've already made the reservation."

I wish I could strangle him, Parker thought. Of course he could simply say he was too busy getting ready to leave, but something warned him to be careful and to go along with Len's unwanted farewell.

Even though it was perfect sailing weather and he spent all day Sunday on the boat, he was not able to enjoy the feel of the water's spray, the gliding of the boat through the water, the clear blue sky, the occasional drifting cloud. Everything was anticipation of the final meeting with Len. He had hoped that it would rain on Monday, a steady persistent rain, but of course it could not have been a more perfect day.

At nine A.M. the foursome teed off. Parker liked the two men who accompanied Len. Bruce Groom was a retired executive in one of the drug companies; quiet, intent on his game, he said very little. Parker had the feeling Bruce did not have the slightest interest in Len's comparison of George Hawkins to Parker Bennett.

Dewayne Lamparello rounded out the foursome. He had the highest handicap of the group but even that could not help his game. Quite simply, he was a lousy golfer, far less interested in inane chatter than seeing that his next shot was not another ground ball.

Len did not bring up the subject of Parker Bennett at all. Parker was beginning to relax, and by the time they sat down to lunch, he was sure he didn't have to worry anymore.

As was to be expected, Len led the conversation. He had been a minor executive in a cereal company.

"I used to say my nickname was 'Snap, crackle, pop,' " he joked, referring to the famous tagline of a Kellogg cereal.

Snap, crackle, shut up, Parker thought, but admitted to himself that he would much prefer this tedious chatter to a replay of a discussion about Parker Bennett.

But when the others ordered a second coffee, he decided he could gracefully get away.

"Well, I really do have to get going," he said. "Len, I think this was great and I thank you. I am sure you understand that I've got quite a checklist to go over before my departure."

"Are you going to rent the house?" Len asked. "Because if you are, I know someone in the market for a good rental."

"No, I am not," Parker replied. "I want to know it's available to me any time I can get away."

"You could do a week-to-week," Len persisted. "You would make a lot of money."

"Again, I have thought about it but have absolutely decided against it," Parker said firmly.

As he stood up to leave he smiled warmly.

"Thanks so much, Len. Bruce, Dewayne, great to play with you again. I hope to see you on the links when I get back. Len, next time lunch is on me." Careful not to seem too hurried, Parker turned toward the exit of the dining room. He had just reached the door when Len shouted, "Hey, Parker."

He spun around and realized too late he had been trapped. In an instant he tried to make a recovery.

With a hearty laugh, he shouted back, "You and your jokes, Len."

The other diners had looked up. How many of them would make the connection? Parker spent the rest of the afternoon willing himself to remain calm while fully expecting a knock on the door and the arrival of the police. But no one came and at eight o'clock the next morning, he was on his way to the airport.

The plane to Miami was leaving on time. As he showed his boarding pass to the attendant, he thought with regret that this would be the last time he was able to fly using the name George Hawkins. He prob-

ably would never set foot in St. Thomas
again.

46

At the insistence of her cousins, Eleanor and Frank Becker made the forty-minute drive from Yonkers to New City in Rockland County for Thanksgiving dinner. Her cousin Joan was her age. Joan's husband, Eddie, was a retired detective. Their two children along with their spouses and four grandchildren made for a festive group.

Eleanor knew it was good for her and Frank to have decided to visit them instead of staying home for another solitary holiday. She liked Joan's family and could feel the sincerity in the warmth with which they greeted her and Frank.

At dinner they studiously avoided any reference to the current situation. It was only when the children had left the table and the adults were lingering over a cup of coffee that the subject was broached.

It was Eleanor who brought it up.

"I know you're all too polite to ask but I

think you may be interested in this." She told them about going under hypnosis and how far she had gotten in trying to remember the name she had seen on that British driver's license.

"The first name was George," she said firmly. "But I simply cannot remember the last name."

"It could make all the difference in the world," Eddie commented. "I know about that from when I was in the department. Of course I never worked that area. I was on the street doing undercover work."

"What's it like to be hypnotized?" Joan asked.

"It wasn't so bad," Eleanor answered. "In fact, it was kind of peaceful, and trust me, the way things are going these days, sometimes I think that I wouldn't mind being hypnotized all the time."

"You'd get sick of going up and down in the elevator," Frank said wryly. It was the first time in months Eleanor had heard him joke about anything.

Maybe if I could just not be so tense all the time, she thought. Maybe I could *make* myself remember.

It was reassuring to have Eddie tell her, "Eleanor, I know how you must be feeling. I have seen innocent people under a cloud of suspicion by the authorities living in a constant state of fear. When are you going back to the hypnotist?"

"I am not sure," she said. "I know how disappointed they were in me. Maybe I just told them something because I wanted to be able to tell them something. Frank, remember when you got stopped in the car because the cop said you had gone through a red light in Manhattan?"

"I remember," Frank said angrily. "I didn't go through any red light. It was still on yellow. That cop had a quota to fill; that's why I was stopped."

"Frank, I've heard that song before," Eddie commented.

"Well, what I mean is when the cop asked Frank for his driver's license, he gave him his credit card by mistake. For a minute he thought Frank was trying to bribe him."

"He must have been a real rookie," Eddie observed dryly. "You don't try to bribe a cop with a credit card."

"The reason I remember," Eleanor continued, "is because maybe I'm mixing up seeing him give the wrong card to the cop with what I think happened in Parker Bennett's office. The point is I don't think it will do any good to go back to the hypnotist. Actually, being hypnotized wasn't a bad experience. It's dreading doing it, then making a fool of myself. When I look back on it, I really don't like being out of control. It was scary somehow to know someone is exploring your mind, and you're giving answers that perhaps aren't even true but just made up."

"I think you're making a mistake, Eleanor," Eddie said quietly. "No one is expecting you to be able to give a complete picture. That would be totally unrealistic. Why don't you go back to that doctor? You have nothing to lose and certainly nothing to fear."

His concern and warmth made Eleanor realize how foolish she had been to withdraw so completely from her immediate circle of family and friends. She had been so sure that under a veneer of sympathy they were judging her as being a part of Parker's elaborate scheme. Over these past two years the newspapers had alleged that she was in on the fraud. Some pretty convincing editorials had been published. "There had to have been another person involved in the fraud," the newspapers had screamed over and over again. She spoke of that now to Joan and Eddie.

"Anyone who knows me well enough would know that I was not capable of being the other person behind that fraud," she said sadly.

And then the inevitable question came. "What about Eric?"

Eleanor answered slowly, "I saw absolutely no indication that he was involved. They have not found one penny in his name that he could not prove had been earned honestly. I know he was very close to his father, but nobody was more shocked and upset when all of this came out than Eric. He broke down and cried in front of me, and believe me, that emotion was genuine. No one is *that* good an actor."

A short time later, as they were getting their coats on to start for home, Eddie spoke softly.

"Eleanor, please accept my advice. Go back to that hypnotist. Please. You will be doing yourself a favor. Again, you have nothing to lose. I know what I'm talking about. Do it for yourself. Do it for Frank. Please."

"Maybe I will," she said hesitantly. "Let me think about it."

47

On Monday morning Lane arrived at the office to find Glady in a foul mood.

"I'm beginning to wonder if La-di-da is running out of cash," was her greeting to Lane. "She owes us two million dollars more, and stupidly I put those paintings and sculptures in the apartment before I got paid for them. Lane, I'm telling you that lady is cash poor."

"Then why on earth did she sign up for five million dollars' worth of interior decorating?" Lane asked incredulously.

"I think because she was so used to having an unending source of cash," Glady answered. "And now maybe it's drying up."

"But if Parker is supporting her, he got away with over five billion dollars. Surely five million is nothing to him," Lane argued.

"Well, two million dollars is a lot to me," Glady snapped, and looked down at her desk, indicating that Lane should clear out of the office.

What a day this is going to be, Lane thought. She knew that when Glady was upset she took it out on everyone around her.

An hour later Glady went out to the reception area and screamed at Vivian because her desk looked as if she was "camping out on it."

Lane knew that Vivian had been given the job of cutting out pictures of celebrity homes so that Glady could keep up to date with what other designers were doing.

Fortunately for Lane, Glady sent her out to one of the smaller jobs, supervising the installation of window treatments and furniture at the newly renovated executive office of the CEO of a food chain.

It was a windy, cold day again, and as Lane supervised the job, her mind was ceaselessly filled with random thoughts about Ken.

The anniversary of Ken's death was next week. Probably that was why her memories were so distinct. She thought of their wedding at Saint Malachy's, the so-called actors' chapel on Forty-Ninth Street in the theater district of Manhattan. She could vividly see herself at the altar exchanging vows with him. Her mother had wanted her

to be married at their church in Georgetown.

I turned her down flat, Lane remembered.
I certainly didn't want to walk down the
aisle on Dwight's arm. That's another way I
slammed my mother in the teeth. I wore a
simple white dress. Ken wore a business
suit, and we had dinner for thirty friends
after the ceremony. My mother came alone.
Dwight was away, but she knew I didn't
want him there.

Another thought that kept churning in her
mind was that she and her mother had been
very close in those ten years after her father
had died. That had all ended when Dwight
came into their lives. She wished she could
put these thoughts out of her head. But she
again wondered how she would feel if Katie,
at age seventeen, for some reason, began to
reject her. The trip to Washington had
opened a door that she was not happy to go
through. She was not able to dislodge those
thoughts.

It was with a sense of anticipation that
evening that Lane left Katie with Wilma at
six o'clock and started to drive to New
Jersey. This time she met Eric at Bella
Gente, in Verona, the next town over from
Montclair. He had asked her on their first
date if she liked Italian food. She had

answered with a completely truthful yes. When she and Glady took a client out to lunch, Glady always chose a high-end New York restaurant. Lane would never have dreamed of telling her that she and maybe even the client would have much preferred a plate of pasta with a simple tomato and basil sauce to any of the signature dishes on the menus of those establishments. She thoroughly despised truffles, which seemed to be the favorite food of so many sophisticated diners. But it had seemed easy to her to confess that to Eric, who had laughingly agreed. He felt the same way.

Eric was already there, seated at a table under a window. He sprang to his feet when he saw her, and taking both her hands in his, he kissed her lightly on the cheek.

"I've missed you," he said. "How was Washington?"

Lane was acutely aware that she didn't want to refer to Dwight in any way.

"We had a very nice time," she answered. "It's such fun to show Katie Washington. After all, I did live there for the first seventeen years of my life."

"I did a lot of going back and forth to Washington myself. When I was with Morgan Stanley we had a pretty sizable list of clients there. I was in the Compliance

266

Department for about ten years and then got into trading."

He was looking straight at her. "Lane, you look so lovely. I have missed you terribly. I've never felt this way about a woman before, and that's all I'll say on the subject. How is Katie doing?"

From the town house next door to Anne Bennett's, FBI agent Jonathan Pierce, alias Tony Russo, had overheard Anne Bennett on the phone with her son. He knew that he and Lane Harmon had decided they were going to Bella Gente tonight but it would be too much of a coincidence for him to show up at the same restaurant.

Jack Keane, another agent, was at the table next to Lane and Eric, a listening device pointed directly at them. He heard Eric tell Lane that his mother did not seem to be feeling very well, although she refused to go to a doctor.

"I'm worried about her," Eric said. "I can't make her go to a doctor. She can be very stubborn."

When Keane reported back to Jonathan at the end of the evening, his report was succinct: "Nothing but the usual dinner chatter. He's very into her and even told her he never felt this way about anybody before. She seemed pretty happy to be with him.

267

After dinner they left in separate cars. I guess she was on her way home."

Though encouraged by the report that they had left separately, Jonathan was still dismayed to hear of Lane's obvious pleasure at being in Eric's company.

48

Sylvie had brushed up on anything she could learn about what Barclay Cameron had been doing in the nearly ten years since she had had an affair with him.

She had heard that he had invested in a number of movies that had bombed. She wasn't sure if she should ask about that.

At six thirty Robert announced his arrival. Sylvie had not run into Barclay in the last few years and had heard he spent a lot of time in California.

When Robert escorted him in, Sylvie was shocked to see how much older he looked. His hand had a slight tremor and he was using a cane. Still, it was with the same courtly manner that he kissed her hand, and in that same well-bred voice he said, "Sylvie, you look absolutely enchanting."

Over the next half hour and before they went off to Marea, Barclay told her of his experiences in Hollywood and inside stories of some of the directors and actors he had met. "It's the essence of phoniness out there, but stimulating enough that I didn't mind the cost."

But then he added, "Even so, I felt quite alone and remembered our little love affair of some years ago. Sylvie, you are by far the most interesting woman I know and to be quite honest, I have missed you very much. I know of course you were involved with Parker Bennett. But now that he is dead, or at least has disappeared, I would like to see if we could rekindle the passion we once felt."

Over dinner Barclay shared memories she had heard before, of his being born on the Lower East Side long before it had become a fashionable place to live and of going to college at night while he sold Atlas elevator shoes in the daytime.

"The shoes had two-inch heels," he said. "So it made the short guys look taller. The company went out of business long ago. I hated that job so much that to this day the sight of an ad for shoes makes me cringe."

Sylvie glanced down and noticed that the fine Italian leather shoes he was wearing were a sharp contrast to the ones he had described.

She had always made it her business to

keep up with the stock market. When she switched the subject to the market, Barclay was in his element. It was easy to feed him questions and she could plainly see that he was as sharp and informed as ever. It was also clear to her that he was enjoying himself.

Over espresso he asked her point-blank, "Sylvie, are you ready to resume our relationship?"

She did not rush to say yes but made herself seem hesitant.

Disappointment in his eyes, Barclay asked, "Sylvie, do you still have feelings for Parker Bennett?"

"Absolutely not!" She shook her head adamantly.

"Good," he replied. "I never quite liked him, although I must say I thought he was a man of financial integrity. It is simply appalling to me that he could cheat so many people of limited income."

"When I think of what he did to all those people it makes me cry," Sylvie agreed. "You certainly know that I did not come from a privileged background. I can only imagine my family being cheated by him."

"That's what I like about you," Barclay said. "It's refreshing. All too often I see that so many of my friends who did come from a privileged background have a sense of entitlement that comes as naturally to them as breathing." He hesitated, then added, "Sylvie, you haven't answered my question. I remember how lovely it was to share what we shared."

"Barclay," she said quietly, "I would be very interested in beginning again."

Declining a nightcap at her apartment, Barclay said, "I will call you tomorrow in the afternoon. I have a board meeting in the morning." His kiss lingered on her lips. "My future wife," he said, then he was gone.

After he left Sylvie went into her study and poured herself a stiff nightcap. She sat for a long time staring straight ahead while sipping her martini. Barclay was not only ready to resume their relationship but wanted to marry her.

Barclay had been married for fifty years to the same woman. Their little fling had happened after his wife died. He had never had children. If I married him, I'd be set for the rest of my life and then some, she thought.

But she did know that if Barclay ever found out that she had been supported these past two years by money Parker had stolen, it would be the end of their relationship. And so what if Parker had finally come through with the last two million? The appointment she had made with Derek Landry was on Friday. In the morning she would call his office and ask if he could see her immediately.

49

Derek Landry's law offices were located in a new skyscraper east of Times Square. Derek had agreed to Sylvie's request to come in earlier, even though it would be necessary to rearrange his schedule, as he had pointed out.

Which means he'll charge me extra for it, she thought.

His law office occupied three floors of the building. The reception area was located on the fortieth floor. Large, with comfortable leather sofas and chairs. A stack of newspapers was piled neatly on a coffee table. I wonder who bothers to read them? she thought.

The shade of light gray paint on the walls made a nice contrast with the deeper gray tones of the carpeting.

The young woman at the reception desk was quietly poised and greeted Sylvie with a smile.

"Mr. Landry is expecting you. I'll have someone escort you up to his office."

Instantly a young man who looked like he was just out of law school was by her side, whisking her into the private elevator and up the two floors to the executive offices.

He led her down a hallway to a conference room with a long table, four chairs on either side and one each at the head and foot.

Sylvie dropped her dark sable jacket on the chair beside her. Another assistant appeared, a woman who looked to be about fifty or so years old. Conservatively dressed in a dark blue jacket and matching slacks, she offered Sylvie coffee, tea, and water. "Just water," Sylvie said, her mouth suddenly dry. A few minutes later Derek Landry appeared in the doorway and in an instant was standing over her, taking her hand in his.

"My dear Countess, a pleasure to see you again. I believe we have met at several charitable functions in the past."

Derek was a tall, very broad man. He was balding, and his face had an almost cherubic look. His eyes were light green, almost gray. His tone was warm and welcoming, but Sylvie knew that by reputation he was a lawyer who got what he wanted for his clients.

During the night Sylvie had carefully planned her presentation.

"Derek, you are aware of what is called Stockholm syndrome?"

"Of course." His tone was noncommittal.

"Let me put it this way. For eight years before he disappeared, Parker Bennett and I were very close friends."

"I understand."

"When he vanished off the face of the earth, I was horrified to learn that he was a treacherous and deceitful human being. Certainly not the man I thought I loved," Sylvie said quietly. "I believed like so many people that Parker was dead. I could not imagine him in a prison cell." She turned away, blinking to make her eyes appear moist. With a sigh, she turned back to face him.

"You can understand my astonishment and horror when I received a phone call from him."

"You received a phone call from Parker Bennett?" Derek's voice was incredulous.

"Yes. He told me that he was living under an assumed identity. He warned me that he would not tolerate my breaking off our relationship. He said that no one else would ever have me. He told me he was going to continue to send me money and expensive gifts, and that I was obliged to accept them. The last time he stayed with me, just before he disappeared, he left a phone in my nightstand with a note that said, 'Keep charged.' "

"Have you told any of this to the police?" Derek asked.

"No, I did not," Sylvie replied.

"Why not?"

"Because I was confused. I did not know what to do."

"Did you keep the phone charged?" Derek asked.

"Yes, I did. He told me to."

"Then you are telling me that Parker Bennett has been in touch with you over these past two years?" Derek persisted.

"Yes."

"And has he been sending you money and gifts?"

"Yes."

"I am not quite sure how I can be of assistance to you, Countess," Derek said curtly.

"You don't know how frightened I have been these past two years. Parker warned me against ever seeing anyone else. He threatened my life. I felt as though every minute I was outside of my apartment I might be in mortal danger."

Sylvie's voice was shaking.

"What do you want from me, Countess?"

"I want you to negotiate with the FBI. I could give them Parker Bennett's new identity, cell phone number, and where he lives. I would insist on receiving the two-million-dollar reward and being granted both anonymity and immunity, full immunity from prosecution. I cannot live this way any longer." Her voice had stopped shaking and turned to steel.

"That is a pretty tall order, Countess," Landry remarked. "You have been living on the proceeds of his theft and you have been protecting his identity."

"And I have always felt a sniper was watching me," she responded angrily.

"Of course this will require *very* delicate negotiations. There is always the chance the FBI is closer to apprehending Parker Bennett than we know. If they *do* apprehend him, it is quite possible he would involve you in any confession he makes."

"I am aware of that," Sylvie said. "That's why this is something that I have to do immediately."

"And you would still demand the reward money?"

"I expect your fee to be high, Derek," she replied. "I am running low on cash. I need the certainty of being able to pay you."

"That is very admirable of you, Countess," Landry said, his voice now smooth.

Sylvie, who could always detect the slightest note of sarcasm, knew she was hearing it now.

"Derek, you have the reputation of being very successful in getting your clients a very favorable outcome, sometimes unfairly, I might add, but that's why I am here. Do we understand each other?"

Derek Landry smiled. "We understand each other perfectly, Countess. I will arrange the contract. My retainer is two hundred thousand dollars."

50

Ranger sat in the living room in Dr. Sean Cunningham's home. Sean had called him and said he was having a meeting of some of the victims of the fraud — a kind of support group. "It gives everyone an opportunity to be heard."

The last thing in the world Ranger wanted to do was to go to Cunningham's home and exchange sad stories with other people. His own story was the only one he was interested in but he sensed that Dr. Cunningham was worried about him.

If he only knew, Ranger thought. If he only knew.

He didn't want Sean to get even a hint of what he was planning. Sean was a psychiatrist. He might be able to get me committed, Ranger thought. He might say that I am a danger to society. He had read about cases like that.

I am not a danger to society, he thought.

Only to a few people who deserve it.

He listened as the others spoke. One couple who were well into their eighties said they had had to move into their son's home after they had lost everything. The wife was speaking. "I always got along so well with my daughter-in-law. But it's different now. My husband and I are both hard of hearing. We always have the volume turned up too high on the television. Sometimes they go out at night just to get away from us. There's nothing we can do." Her voice broke. "There's nothing we can do."

At least you still have each other, Ranger thought bitterly.

It reminded Ranger of when he and Judy visited Parker Bennett's office. Comfortable chairs, not formal or anything. Parker would have his secretary bring in a tray of coffee and assorted muffins. While they were eating they would listen to Parker as he boasted that he was the broker for people who did not understand the financial world. He would see to it that they would be comfortable in their retirement years, far more comfortable than what their savings could yield in the bank at a mere 1 or 2 percent interest.

Ranger could still see Judy smiling gratefully at Parker, flattered that he had taken them on as clients. She had dared to dream of a future of comfort and security with Ranger and perhaps some small luxuries.

After we signed up with him, we kept putting more and more of our savings into his fund. We economized. We *saved* to give him more money. A small sacrifice now for a wonderful payday down the road; that's what we believed. That was what he convinced us it would be.

The voices had begun again. Voices sometimes soothing, often terrifying. He remembered first hearing them when he was a teenager. At times they roared at him like a howling beast from hell. Then Judy came into his life. His beloved Judy. The voices had dulled and then gone silent. He had thought they were gone forever but then they came back. He wondered what Dr. Cunningham's reaction would be if he knew that he kept a loaded gun in his apartment.

He had come to like the feel of the gun in his hands. He had practiced loading and unloading it. For the past week he had been going to a shooting range. He was sure that by now he was as good a shot as any cop on the force.

When it was Ranger's turn to speak he did his best to keep the bitterness out of his voice. He told the group about Judy's stroke. "It happened just days after we found out that we had been wiped out.

"I used to carry her in my arms to the bathroom," he whispered. "I didn't mind. I loved her. I would have done anything for her. My only prayer was that she would stay with me. Then a month ago she had another stroke and died."

"She couldn't stay with you, Ranger," Sean interjected gently. "She was just too ill."

"I wanted to be close to Judy so I put her ashes in something I could wear around my neck," he continued, watching the unwanted sympathy in the expressions of his listeners. "But now I only wear it at night. That way I don't feel so alone."

Cunningham was nodding like he was approving of what he was saying.

If you only knew, doctor. Ranger closed his lips to stop the laugh he could feel coming on.

The last member of the group was finishing his boring story. Some old guy, he was so broke that Meals on Wheels brought him breakfast and dinner five days a week.

When it was time to go Ranger thanked Dr. Cunningham and assured him again that he was doing well. It was ten minutes of five. In another ten minutes Eric Bennett would be leaving his office. A couple of times now Ranger had watched from down the block to see Eric coming in the morning and leaving in the afternoon. Eric's apartment was not far from his office. He usually walked to and from work.

I could pick him off any time I wanted, Ranger thought. But that would be a mistake. I'd never get a chance at his mother. They're living on my money right now. Mine and Judy's. The anger inside him was again boiling over.

When he went outside there was a light snow falling. He liked the feel of it under his shoes. He barely noticed the people who were on the street hurrying home at the end of the day. He was walking toward Eric Bennett's office building. He stood outside it. Fifteen minutes later Eric came out the revolving door. Ranger let him get half a block ahead and then began to follow him.

This time Eric didn't go straight home to his apartment. He stopped at a bar on West Thirteenth Street and was joined by a couple of men his age. Peering through the window Ranger watched as they laughed together.

Having a good time? He seethed. Not for much longer, I promise you. Not for much longer. He walked the two miles back to his apartment. Without taking off his coat, he sat down on his couch. Eric is staying in the city tonight. That means he'll go visit his mother tomorrow night, Ranger reasoned. I'll park down the block from his garage and follow him to New Jersey.

It's fun to follow him, a voice whispered. His father had control of you and every dollar you ever saved but now you have control of him. Whenever you want you can aim the gun at him and watch him die.

Ranger realized he had not taken off his still-damp overcoat. He got up, shrugged out of it, and dropped it on the couch.

He hadn't eaten any lunch but he wasn't hungry. Judy never drank. When she was alive he had had only the occasional beer or scotch. Now he got up, walked into the kitchen to get a glass, and opened a bottle of scotch. He sat down again on the couch and poured the scotch into the glass. He filled it to the top. There was even a little that spilled over on the table. He began to drink.

Two hours later, the bottle empty, he fell asleep on the couch, his still-damp overcoat covering him.

51

On Tuesday night Ranger followed Eric's car to New Jersey. To his surprise Eric did not drive to his mother's house but instead turned off the highway in a town called Verona and stopped at a restaurant.

He doesn't know me, Ranger thought. I can eat dinner here. I'm dressed okay.

He went into the restaurant. He could see into the dining room where Eric was sitting. He asked the hostess for a corner table near the window. That way he would be able to see Eric knowing that if he wanted to, he could kill him right now.

A couple of minutes later a really good-looking broad joined Eric. With loathing, Ranger watched as Eric stood up and kissed her. Was she the one in the car that day when he was driving past his mother's town house? he wondered. When Eric and this girlfriend sat down they began smiling and talking while he sat alone. He noticed another man by himself at a table near them. The rest of the room was filling with couples and small groups. Everyone appeared to be having a real good time and real thrilled to be together. The more people that came in, the lonelier and angrier he felt. He did not taste his meal; his focus was on Eric and his girlfriend.

When Eric signaled for his check, Ranger did the same. He had parked his car across the street. He sure wasn't going to bring his old wreck to be valet parked. Then, sitting in it, he watched as the valet pulled up with the girlfriend's car first and then Eric's. Ranger was surprised to see them in separate cars.

He followed the girlfriend as she drove into Manhattan and watched her pull into the garage at 240 West Fifty-Sixth Street.

He was about to drive away when he saw her coming up the ramp. Where is she going? He was planning to follow her but then she walked to the very next building and the doorman stepped aside to let her in.

Nice building. We never had a doorman. But you have one. Maybe Eric's paying for your apartment. He bought you a fancy dinner, but it was on me.

Ranger's anger had a new target.

The pretty young woman with long red-

dish hair who had been grinning happily at
Eric Bennett.

52

Rudy Schell received an interesting phone call from a lawyer he knew by reputation and did not like. He considered Derek Landry the kind of attorney who gave the legal profession a bad name. Landry had represented many high-powered people who got in trouble taking or giving kickbacks. He had an astonishingly high success rate at getting his clients exceptionally good deals.

To receive a phone call from him was an unwelcome surprise. Landry was asking for a meeting on a most urgent matter, a matter he knew Rudy would be keenly interested in. "It concerns Parker Bennett."

It was an effort for Rudy to keep his voice noncommittal. "I certainly will make time for you, Mr. Landry. When would you like to meet?"

"This afternoon."

"Three o'clock?" Rudy suggested.

"See you then."

When Derek Landry arrived at Rudy's promptly at the stroke of three, Rudy took him into one of the private offices used for face-to-face meetings.

He closed the door and gestured for Derek to sit down.

"What can I do for you, Mr. Landry?" he asked.

"This is a very delicate matter," Landry replied, his tone hushed. "I have a client who is most reliable, who will be able to assist you in locating Parker Bennett."

"Reliable?" Rudy asked.

"Absolutely. But we insist on complete anonymity. I am not authorized to provide details unless and until you express interest in our proposal. My client also wants the reward money and a guarantee of full immunity from prosecution. I can assure you that my client played no role whatsoever in the Parker Bennett fraud scheme. My client, under threat from Parker Bennett, has been forced to accept a very small percent of the proceeds of the fraud after Mr. Bennett disappeared."

"What you are asking for is a tall order, Mr. Landry. Ordinarily I would have to know the name of your client before considering your offer. If your client's role is exactly as you describe it, then yes, I will consider it. And as I am sure you know, a decision such as this must go through the highest channels before an answer can be given."

"Of course." Derek smiled. "I hope to hear from you soon, Mr. Schell. I will see myself out."

53

On Wednesday morning Lane went to work, her mind filled with what Eric had told her the night before. Once again, it had been so very pleasant. She could not deny the chemistry that was developing between them. In this past week alone the attraction between them had grown ever stronger. She certainly felt it and she was sure it was not one-sided. Once again he had expressed his feelings for her. Yet so many people thought he had been involved with his father in the theft.

Dwight absolutely despised him. But why? It wasn't fair that he would never give any reason for feeling that way.

I can't love somebody and get hurt again, she thought, remembering the heartbreak of losing her father and then Ken. Katie can't get hurt either. Even though Katie had not seen Eric for several weeks, she had asked about him just this morning.

But fortunately, Glady's mood had improved greatly.

"I can have the art and sculptures picked up from La-di-da's apartment if I don't receive her payment," she said. "It's absolutely against the policy of the Greer Company to take back anything they sold, but they recognize the fact that I have purchased there for many clients over the years."

"I'm so glad. That was really nice of them," Lane said enthusiastically.

"Well it certainly doesn't hurt them to cut me some slack. They've made a fortune on the people I've brought there," Glady said. "I've earned every cent. That dump was a cluttered mess, a tribute to bad taste, until I got my hands on it."

I think I've heard that before, Lane thought, but she did agree and gave Glady the reassurance she wanted. "Glady, it's one of your finest projects. That apartment is inviting and beautiful."

Later that day they were in the office when a phone call came in from FBI agent Rudy Schell asking both of them to please come into his office at their earliest convenience.

Holding the phone in her hand, Glady went into Lane's office. "An FBI agent wants to see us," she said. "Have you any appointments tomorrow?"

"Nothing I can't change," Lane answered.

"Well this should be interesting," Glady said. "I'll bet my next commission check that this is about Her Royal Nothing, the countess, and I also bet it has something to do with Parker Bennett."

"I wouldn't be surprised," Lane said even as she feared it might also be about Eric.

"And didn't I say she still may be involved with him?" Glady continued. "Didn't I tell you that?"

"Yes you did, Glady. Yes you did."

That evening over dinner Katie told Lane about how her teacher told her that she was going to be a wonderful artist someday. "That's what I tell you, Katie!" Lane said, hoping her daughter would not notice how preoccupied she was.

"And I have a special surprise for you and I want to show you right now," Katie said excitedly. "May I please?"

"Of course." Lane smiled indulgently.

She listened to Katie's hurried footsteps as she ran down the hallway to her room. When she returned, she was holding a piece of canvas about the size of a legal envelope.

"Let me see," Lane said, a genuine smile on her face.

She looks so much like Ken, Lane thought

as Katie hugged the canvas with a happy smile. Of course that red hair is from my side but her eyes and the shape of her face are just like his. The anniversary of his death was only a few days away. Her mind continued to be filled with the memories of their brief life together and what might have been if he had lived.

Then slowly, dramatically, Katie turned the canvas and proudly displayed it.

"Does it look like Daddy?" she asked excitedly. "I took the picture from your dresser to school with me every day last week but I brought it home every day and put it right back. That was okay, wasn't it?"

Lane stared, unable to speak over the lump in her throat. It was certainly a child's artistic re-creation but it was Ken just the same.

"It's beautiful," she whispered. "It looks just like him. He would be so proud of you."

"Am I like him?" Katie asked, her voice suddenly wistful.

"Yes, you are." Lane stood up, folded her in her arms, careful not to crush the precious canvas. Then she took it from Katie and laid it carefully at the end of the table.

When they both sat down and began to eat, she said, "Your daddy used to tell me that when he was your age, he loved to draw and paint. I still have a few pictures that he did when he was in the first grade. I'm going to find them and show them to you."

Later, when Katie was in bed, Lane sat in the living room with no desire to turn on the television. She had an unsettled feeling because the timing of this picture just before the anniversary of Ken's death was coupled with trying to sort out her feelings about Eric. Where was all of this going? What would Ken think about her relationship with Eric? Was Eric the kind of man Ken would approve of as a stepfather for Katie? She knew it was inevitable that if she kept seeing Eric their relationship would move to the next level.

Last night was proof of that. At the end of their dinner Eric told her again how much he cared about her.

"Lane, I'm thirty-seven years old," he began. "I've had my share of relationships. But there was always something missing. I've always known something more was waiting for me.

"And now, with you, I've found it."

54

Once again Lane did not sleep very well that night. The next afternoon, at three o'clock, she and Glady arrived at Rudy Schell's office.

Rudy escorted them into one of the conference rooms and, after offering them coffee, came right to the point.

"Ms. Harper," he said to Glady. "How much longer will you be working at Countess de la Marco's apartment?"

"It will be another few weeks before the last of the details are completed," Glady answered.

"Has she been paying you regularly?" Rudy continued.

"She was. But she owes me two million dollars now. She claims she'll have it in a few days. I can tell she's stalling for time. If she doesn't come through very soon, I'm having some paintings and sculptures removed, and that of course lowers my commission." Glady's tone was clearly annoyed.

Rudy nodded. "The fact that she may be running out of cash is exactly what I expected to hear," he said, a note of satisfaction in his voice.

"And why is that?" Glady asked. "Are you a mind reader?"

Always that touch of sarcasm with Glady, Lane thought.

"I wish I were a mind reader. I could have solved many cases a lot faster and with a lot less hard work." Rudy's tone was business-like. "Ms. Harper, Ms. Harmon, are you aware that the countess was rumored to be Parker Bennett's mistress?"

"Rumored!" Glady laughed. "Of course she was. Everybody knows that."

"Parker Bennett's body was never found but we think it is entirely possible, even probable, that he staged his disappearance. I understand that you have been in and out of her apartment regularly these past weeks. Do you think she might have been in touch with Bennett?"

"I wouldn't be at all surprised," Glady answered. "The first time I told her how much it would cost to decorate the apartment, she excused herself and left the room to make a phone call. When she came back, she gave us the go-ahead. I think she was talking to her version of Santa Claus."

"Good analogy," Rudy observed. "Then you do believe it's a possibility?"

"Possibility, sure. Probability, maybe," Glady replied.

"Recently on Page Six in the *Post* there was an item about the countess having dinner with Barclay Cameron," Rudy said.

"You read the *Post*," Glady commented. "I would think you were too busy to waste time on Page Six. I saw that item as well. The countess and Barclay Cameron were an item some years ago. My guess is she's trying to rekindle the flame because something has happened to her cash flow."

"Ms. Harper, you seem to be very knowledgeable about the countess's activities," Schell observed dryly.

"When you are an interior designer for the kind of clientele I have, you hear a great deal of gossip," Glady snapped.

Schell turned to Lane. "Ms. Harmon, you have been seeing Eric Bennett?"

Astonished, Lane said, "I have had dinner with him a few times. Why do you care about that?"

"I have made it my business to be aware of Bennett's activities and now I will tell you both why I asked you here today. We believe we may be getting closer to apprehending Parker Bennett. We believe the countess is in touch with him. We have always believed that Eric Bennett was involved in his father's fraud."

"And he has been living with the knowledge that many people believe that, Mr. Schell," Lane argued. "It has been a terrible burden for him to bear."

"Maybe, maybe not," Rudy replied. "The point is that each of you can be of great service to the FBI. Let me put it another way. If we apprehend Parker Bennett, we believe we would be able to recover at least some, if not most, of the money he stole. Ms. Harper, like you, we think the countess is communicating with Parker Bennett. I would like you to continue to go in and out of that apartment as often as is reasonable and report to us anything you may hear. Obviously you do feel the countess is getting nervous about the decorating expenses."

"You bet she is," Glady retorted. "Like I said, I plan on removing some artwork and sculptures from the apartment unless the outstanding two million dollars is paid this week."

"Wouldn't that terminate your relationship with the countess?" Rudy asked worriedly.

"Yes, it would, because I sure as heck am not going to do any more work if I'm not getting paid," Glady answered.

"Ms. Harper," Rudy began slowly, "would you leave the artwork there so that you can continue to frequent the apartment for a while longer? I would like you to place a listening device in the countess's bedroom. I assure you I have a court order authorizing this. During the day when she is not there, what room does she spend most of her time in?"

"The library," Glady answered. "She usually has her lunch served in there and whenever she takes a phone call, she does so in that room."

"Then I will want a listening device in the library as well," Rudy said. "And, Ms. Harmon, I would like you to encourage Eric Bennett in his affection toward you."

"How do you know he shows affection toward me?" Lane asked angrily.

"We have been watching him, Ms. Harmon," Rudy replied. "I would like you to win Eric Bennett's trust. Tell him you don't care if he was involved with his father. At least hint at that."

"I absolutely will do no such thing!" Lane cried. "Eric is a fine and decent man and he has suffered terribly throughout this entire ordeal. He told me he emptied his own bank account and turned over every dime he had to the victims' recovery fund."

Rudy's voice became chipped with ice. "Ms. Harmon, Eric Bennett did not give one penny to the victims' recovery fund. Believe me, I would know. If he told you that, it was a complete fabrication. And if he lied to you about that, I can assure you that he's lied about other things as well. Our hope is that if you seem to him to be responsive to his overtures toward you, if you even tell him you don't care if he was involved in the fraud, he may trust you enough to confide in you. Now I will show you how to use a listening device when you are with him. I would also ask you to see him perhaps several times each week for dinner."

Shaken, Lane stared at Schell. I don't think he's telling the truth, she thought. He's manipulating me to try to get me to spy on Eric; I know he is. The thought of wearing a hidden microphone to record every word Eric said was abhorrent to her.

"I absolutely refuse to cooperate," she said heatedly. "I believe in Eric Bennett's innocence. It's disgusting that you are asking me to entrap him."

"Do you believe that Eric Bennett really

emptied his bank account and sold his stock portfolio to aid the victims?" Schell asked scornfully.

"Yes I do, Mr. Schell, and I believe you are trying to trick me into turning against a friend who trusts me."

"You're a fool, Lane," Glady said crisply. "I will be happy to plant those devices in the countess's apartment, Mr. Schell. As I told you, I believe Parker Bennett's money is paying my bills and I don't like it. If you can prove the countess is involved, you would be able to seize that apartment and its proceeds would go to the victims' fund, correct?"

"That is correct," Rudy agreed.

"Well, you will get more money for it since my refurbishment than you would have before. So that is my contribution to the fund," Glady said.

"Glady, you seem to be forgetting that the de la Marcos' estate owns the apartment, not the countess," Lane interjected.

"I haven't forgotten that, Lane," Glady shot back. "But if she goes to jail, I will bet you that if they can get that apartment back, they will be happy to make some sort of deal to repay the value of my improvements."

Rudy Schell had heard that Glady Harper

was an excellent businesswoman. She sure is, he thought, then said, "Ms. Harper, thank you. With your help we may be able to bring Parker Bennett to justice."

He turned to Lane. "Ms. Harmon, I would be most grateful if you would cooperate with us. I hope you will reconsider."

"I won't," Lane snapped.

She sat quietly while an agent came in and showed Glady how to wear the listening device and where to place one in the library and one in the bedroom of the de la Marco apartment. As she expected, Glady only needed to be told once. When the agent started to go over the process again, she snapped, "I'm not a complete idiot. A child could learn how to do it the first time."

When they were ready to leave, Rudy Schell looked at Lane. "As I said a few minutes ago, I hope you will reconsider and cooperate. It is my obligation to inform you that if you divulge to anyone the existence of the court order authorizing the listening devices, you will be criminally charged with obstruction of justice."

"I will neither say nor hint at any of this." Lane turned and left the room. Glady followed her, silent.

For once she's being smart, Lane thought as they went down in the elevator. She knows better than to make any wisecracks about Eric and me. If she does, she better find herself another assistant. And she'll never find one as good as I am.

Rudy had escorted them to the door of the conference room. Now he sat down. He was absolutely sure that Derek Landry was representing Countess de la Marco and the last thing he wanted was to give her the reward money on top of guaranteed immunity and anonymity. To get Parker Bennett they might have to go along with it but at least they could stall for a little while.

Rudy sensed it was all coming to a head. He felt that rush of excitement that was always part of his nature when he was closing in for the kill. He could taste the satisfaction of knocking on the door of wherever Parker Bennett was hiding and placing him under arrest.

55

During the drive back to Montpelier, Joel Weber took in the surrounding area. The skies were bluer here than in Manhattan. Understandable, he thought. New York has more cars, more buildings, and God knows how many more people.

It was nearly three o'clock when he pulled into the parking lot of Montpelier High School. If it had been very cold in Hanover, it was downright freezing here!

With hurried steps he went from the parking lot to the school and rang the bell. Instantly, a slender woman in her late sixties was at the door pulling it open with one hand.

"Hello, Mr. Weber, I'm Kay Madonna, the principal's secretary. I'll take you right in to him. He's been expecting you."

Joel followed her down the hall through a small reception area and into the office of Glenn Callow. A man of about sixty, of average height and a full head of salt-and-pepper hair, he rose, extended his hand, invited Joel to sit down, then came directly to the point.

"How can I help you, Mr. Weber? What is this about?"

"I'll start out by informing you that I am a retired FBI agent and am now with Adams Investigations Agency. We are looking into the background of Eric Bennett. We have learned that a young woman who graduated from your school was dating him with some regularity before he suddenly left Magna Carta College seventeen years ago. Were you here at that time?" Joel asked.

"Yes, I was."

"It is my understanding that the young woman he was dating was Regina Crowley. Do you remember her?"

"Very well," Callow responded. His face relaxed into a smile. "Regina was an A student, on the debating team, and a good tennis player."

"Did anything out of the ordinary happen to Regina while she was at your school?"

"No, not really."

Joel sensed that Callow was growing uncomfortable with his questions.

"Mr. Callow, please understand that I am only interested in Regina Crowley insofar as she may be linked to Eric Bennett," Joel said.

"I appreciate that, Mr. Weber, but aside from Regina withdrawing during her junior year due to a prolonged case of mononucleosis, I can't think of anything that was unusual during her time here."

"Do you know what happened to her after that?" Joel persisted.

"Yes, I do. She returned to school the following year. After graduating near the top of her class she went to Boston College and BC Law School."

"Have you kept in touch with her?" Joel asked.

"As far as I know she has never been back here," Callow said quietly. "But she does send a donation to the student fund every year."

"Can you give me her address?"

The principal hesitated for a moment. "I don't see any reason why not. Her married name is Fitzsimmons and she lives in Hartford. I should add that she is a real estate attorney with the law firm of Manley and Fusaro. Their offices are located in Hartford."

Joel rose from his chair. He knew that there was no need to ask any more questions of the principal. He had the information he needed from this interview.

"Mr. Callow, you have been most helpful and I am grateful to you for taking the time to see me," Joel said. The two men shook hands and Joel headed out to the parking lot.

As soon as he was in his car he dialed information on his cell phone and asked for the number and address of the Manley & Fusaro law firm. In an instant, a text message had been sent to his phone with the information he needed.

He pressed the call button and when an operator answered, he asked to speak to Regina Fitzsimmons.

"One moment please. I'll see if she's here."

At the first ring, he heard the phone being picked up. "Regina Fitzsimmons," a voice answered.

"Ms. Fitzsimmons, please allow me to introduce myself. My name is Joel Weber. I am a private investigator and a former FBI agent. I would like very much to meet with you. I am investigating the background of Eric Bennett and I believe you may have information which might prove relevant. Would you be willing to see me?" he asked.

There was a long pause. "Finally, after all this time. I guess it won't do any harm. Yes, Mr. Weber, I will see you."

"I am leaving Montpelier now. I understand it is about a three-hour drive to Hartford? I could be at your office at approximately six thirty. Is it possible to meet you then?" Joel replied.

"Yes," Fitzsimmons confirmed. "I'm planning to work late so about six thirty will be fine. Do you have our address?"

"Yes, I do, and thank you very much." Joel broke the connection, thinking what a productive afternoon he had had so far.

A light snow had begun to fall but fortunately he reached Hartford before it grew in intensity and had the chance to become a real winter storm.

The law offices of Manley & Fusaro were located in a solid red brick building on Main Street in Hartford.

Joel parked his car, sprinted up the stairs to the entrance, and rang the bell of the firm.

Joel had calculated that Regina Fitzsimmons was approximately thirty-four years old. The young woman who answered the door was a petite blonde. She looked even younger than Joel had imagined. Her greeting was warm.

"Please come in, Mr. Weber. I'm Regina Fitzsimmons. There's hot coffee waiting in my office. I am sure you could use a cup

310

after such a long drive."

She led Joel through the reception area and into her private office. The receptionist had left for the day but Joel could hear other voices coming from down the hall.

She closed the door, invited him to sit down, and took her own chair at her desk.

"I knew this day would come," she said. "And maybe I'm glad it has. I see Eric has been getting away with helping his father steal all that money and it sickens me."

The story she proceeded to tell Joel was horrifying.

"All of us used to go to the Magna Carta football games. Eric was a sophomore there. I was a junior in high school. He started paying attention to me. He would sit next to me at the games and at halftime he always bought me my favorite game snack, a hot chocolate and a hot pretzel. He was good-looking and very charming. I was flattered and I guess I had a crush on him. One Saturday it was particularly nasty out, cold and rainy, a kind of icy rain. Before the game even started, Eric said to me, 'Let's get out of here and find a movie.' On the way, he stopped at a diner. 'Wait in the car,' he said. 'They may not have a hot pretzel but I can get you a hot chocolate.' He came back carrying the hot chocolate. He urged me to drink it. A few minutes later he said, 'You look pale. Are you okay?' "

Regina stopped and turned her face away from Joel. He could see the tears in her eyes.

Regina continued. "The next thing I knew I was waking up. We were coming out of a drive-in movie. It was three hours later. He said I had fallen asleep for most of the movie. He said, 'I think you're getting sick.' I didn't feel well. I thought I must have been getting my period because later I saw some blood on my underwear. It simply never occurred to me that he had raped me. Six weeks later I started bleeding profusely. My mother rushed me to the hospital and she was told that I had had a miscarriage."

"What was her reaction?" Joel asked quietly.

"Sheer horror," Regina whispered.

"Did she report it to the police?" Joel asked.

"The doctor asked if the sex was consensual and my mother said yes. She gave me a look that would have killed, but I understood. If she had reported a date rape, no matter how hard you try you can't keep that kind of thing a secret. It gets around. She didn't want that to follow me all of my life. But then I guess I had some sort of breakdown. I could not stop crying. I couldn't sleep, couldn't eat," Regina took a deep breath and continued.

"My father abandoned us when I was two years old. I have no idea where he is. My mother was trying to decide if she had made a mistake in not reporting it when she saw the condition I was in. She called her one male relative. He was her cousin Dwight Crowley, the columnist. He came to see us and he was absolutely wonderful. He took me to a psychiatrist who was fabulous. Dwight paid for everything. I told the doctor that the only time I could possibly have conceived was the day Eric gave me a ride from that football game. I simply don't remember the next few hours after I got into his car. The psychiatrist believed I was telling the absolute truth and was not trying to cover up any secret romance. Neither Dwight nor the doctor agreed with my mother about covering it up, but she was just so frantic about my reputation. The psychiatrist, of course, was bound by doctor-patient confidentiality, but Mother made Dwight swear to her he would never tell anyone about it. Our story was simply that I had contracted a severe case of mononucleosis and that was why I lost the school year."

"Do you think everyone believed it?" Joel's

voice was soothing.

"Yes, I do," Regina responded. "And right after all this happened a student at Magna Carta reported to the dean that Eric Bennett had tried to force himself on her but that she had managed to break away from him. That's why he was asked to leave the school. His father made a ten-million-dollar donation so that his record remained unblemished. The story was that Eric left voluntarily when in reality he had been expelled."

"I was told that Eric Bennett was mugged at that time."

Regina was crying now but managed a smile. "I still don't know and will probably never know for certain if Dwight had a hand in that. It could have been someone who knew the other girl he molested. I just don't know."

"Is it all right if I share this information you have given me with my office? You have my word it will not go any further," Joel said.

"As long as I have your word it will remain confidential, then yes. Let me just add that as you may already know, in regard to Eric Bennett, beneath that charming exterior there is a nasty, vicious, dangerous man." Regina's voice rose in anger as she spoke.

"Believe me, Ms. Fitzsimmons, I will not forget. Now, if I may, I have one final question I would like to ask you. Do you by chance know if Eric was close to his father?"

" 'Close' isn't the word," Regina said heatedly. "Eric was always talking about him, bragging about him, telling people how smart he was, how successful he was, how generous he was. Parker Bennett showered Eric with gifts. The car Eric drove me in was a Maserati, a gift from Dad for his birthday."

She paused and then continued. "Mr. Weber, from what I read in the newspapers and from all that I remember about Eric, I would bet those two were joined at the hip cheating those poor people. If you can prove that Eric is involved, I swear, I'll throw a party."

56

Parker Bennett got off the plane in Miami and dragged his two suitcases outside the terminal. On the Internet he had found a Night and Day Motel that was near the airport. It was located in a part of town that he knew was sleazy and where no questions would be asked. He would register under a different name and by paying cash in advance would be safe from detection.

In the bathroom of the airport he had changed from his customary trench coat into a lightweight polyester zip-up jacket. He had also bought a cap, one size larger than he needed, which came down over his eyes and sat low on his forehead. Hailing a cab, he gave the address of the motel.

When he first arrived at the registration desk, he put a one-hundred-dollar-bill on the counter. "For you," he said to the desk clerk. The clerk, a sallow bald guy who looked as though he had seen everything, slid the bill into his pocket and said, "The room is fifty dollars a night, pay in advance."

The bedroom was exactly what he'd expected. It smelled of stale cigarette smoke. The bedspread was grimy and stained. He shuddered to think what had caused those stains. Disgusted, he reminded himself that he would not be here for too long.

He took the threadbare towel from the bathroom, moistened it with tap water, and wiped down the surfaces of the dresser and nightstands. The towel came up black with grit. He had a flashback to the mansion in Greenwich, where in his bedroom the stately mahogany furniture was always glistening, kept immaculately clean by the weekly maid service and the housekeeper.

It will be easy to keep out of sight in a place like this, Parker thought bitterly. Then he reminded himself that once he had gotten the number of that Swiss account and had access to the money, the rest of his life would be smooth sailing, literally!

He threw the dirty towel in the wastebasket and sat down on what passed for the desk chair. He realized that getting up so early to finish his packing and the anxiety of being stopped at any time were contributing to his feelings of exhaustion. He ate dinner that night at a nearby diner, came back to the room at the motel, and slept for ten hours.

The following morning, feeling refreshed, he looked up the number of a nearby passport office and cabbed there. His birth certificate in the name of Joseph Bennett was in his pocket. They're looking for Parker Bennett, not Joseph Bennett. But the moment he spoke to a clerk at the office he realized there was no way he would get a passport. Even with his birth certificate, the clerk informed him he would need three other different forms of identification, including his driver's license, if he had one, and social security card. He took the passport forms, ostensibly to finish the application at home. At the nearest litter basket, he angrily tore them up and threw them in it. At that moment he didn't know what his next move would be.

If Sylvie had turned him in, it would soon be over. Every cop at every airport would be on the lookout for George Hawkins. And then, suddenly, he began to laugh, an almost hysterical laugh. Sylvie had only seen the boat receipt. She didn't know he had a British passport. The Feds would be looking for an American passport — an American passport registered in the name of George Hawkins.

So now I have to hang out here for a while, he thought. I'll buy a gray or white wig, or maybe both. He had always battled with his weight. He had struggled to keep himself at an even two hundred pounds by watching his diet and exercising regularly. Over these next few weeks he would indulge himself. He would welcome some of those pounds he had spent forty years fighting and pack them on while enjoying high-fat, delicious foods.

Waffles and crisp bacon for breakfast, he thought. Thick cheeseburgers and French fries for lunch. Every fattening food I can think of, I will thoroughly enjoy.

Pleased by the thought of the wonderful meals that awaited him, Parker tipped the cabby, who dropped him off in front of the motel.

Home sweet home, he thought, smiling to himself. It shouldn't take more than a few weeks to grow a beard, gain weight, and complete the makeover I need. It will all work out. It has to.

There was one more item on his list. He needed a gun. Not that he intended to use it. He certainly did not plan to kill anyone, but when he did reach Anne's town house, he had to be prepared. If she showed any sign of turning him in, he knew the sight of a gun would terrify her and guarantee her silence.

Sylvie de la Marco — Sally Chico, he thought contemptuously. She had sucked him dry financially these last two years and she was going to get away with it.

Of course, if he was caught, he'd have one consolation. She too would land in prison and he wouldn't be paying millions of dollars to decorate her cell.

57

Eleanor Becker was not surprised to receive a call from Sean Cunningham. He asked her if he could take her and Frank out to lunch.

"I suspect you are not getting out too often these days, Eleanor," he said.

"No, not much," Eleanor had admitted.

Even though it had been less than two weeks, the warmth she had felt at Thanksgiving dinner with her cousins was just that, a memory, and it seemed a distant one. Every morning she awakened with a sense of great weariness. Her dreams were troubled and even frightening. She was being shoved into a dark room, then she realized it was a prison cell. She could see only bars all around her. She began to pound on them. She started crying and shouting, "No, please, let me out of here, please let me out of here. I didn't do it, I swear to you, I didn't do it!!!"

Those nightmares, combined with her ceaseless worry about Frank's diabetes, made her feel as though she was completely hollow inside. When she did leave the house it was only on Sunday morning to go to Mass. As she sat in church she would glance surreptitiously from side to side to see if anyone was staring at her. Even in church, peace escaped her.

Her response to Sean's luncheon invitation was a simple, "I don't think so."

"Well I do," Sean said firmly. "Eleanor, you've got to get out. We'll go to Xaviars. It looks out over the Hudson. The food is delicious. It will do you a world of good. I'll pick you and Frank up at twelve thirty tomorrow."

When Eleanor hung up the phone, she turned to Frank. "It seems as if we've got a lunch date with Sean Cunningham," she said nervously.

"I like him," Frank said decisively. "Maybe he'll convince you to go back to the hypnotist. I certainly hope he can."

The next morning, Eleanor went to the beauty salon. Since all the trouble had started, she had been doing her hair at home except when it absolutely needed to be cut. After she shampooed, she would let it air-dry and then push the naturally wavy tresses around her face, framing her forehead. But it still never looked quite right.

Now, sitting in the beautician's chair, she felt more like herself. She felt more like the secretary who brought coffee and doughnuts for the victims who were unknowingly handing their life savings to Parker Bennett, she thought sadly.

Sean had gotten a table by the window. As he had promised, they could gaze out over the Hudson, which looked cold with whitecaps, in stark contrast to the same river that filled in the summer with private boats.

Sean greeted them and pointed to the river.

A harbinger of things to come," he said. "It's predicted to be a cold, snowy winter and it looks as though it's starting early."

Eleanor seldom had a drink at lunch but with Sean's encouragement, she had a glass of wine and so did Frank. As they ordered, she began to feel her spirits lift just as she had at Thanksgiving. It was good to get out; Sean and Frank had been right.

Over pasta Sean asked her, "Eleanor, I'm sure you remember Ranger Cole. You saw him at the funeral service."

"I remember him, poor man," Eleanor answered. "He looked as though he was totally out of it. I felt sorry for him."

"I'm afraid he is still out of it," Sean said. "He tried to put on a good front at the meeting last week but I could see through it."

Over coffee, Sean broached the subject of the psychiatrist/hypnotist.

"Eleanor, I know how reluctant you are to go back to him. Believe me, I do understand. But you have given the only clue we have to capturing Parker Bennett and that is that he has or had a British driver's license. The FBI has told me how very important it is to have that information and they have it because of you. If you can remember his full name under hypnosis, the FBI has a great chance of closing in on him. That could mean that all of those people whose lives have been so harmed may end up recovering a good portion of the monies they lost. Eleanor, you have got to reconsider." Sean's tone was pleading. "And it will surely help you with your own case."

"I know all that," Eleanor replied. "It's just . . ." She stopped, took a deep breath, and began again.

"I could see how disappointed everyone was when I was there the last time. Then I started to think. Maybe I made it all up. Maybe I didn't see a British license at all and my mind is playing tricks on me. Sean, what if I'm wrong?" Eleanor's voice started to quiver.

"Let the FBI worry about that," Sean responded firmly. "It's up to them to substantiate whether your memory is accurate and it's far better they track down a false lead than if they have nothing at all to work with."

"Eleanor, you know what I've been telling you all along," Frank interjected. "Sean's right. Let the FBI decide what is and is not accurate. Go ahead and do it, honey."

Eleanor smiled, a tentative smile.

"And they won't think I'm making fools of them if I say things that turn out not to be true?" she asked.

"Eleanor, oftentimes under hypnosis, people are able to complete a partial memory. People can recall part of a license plate number when they have witnessed a crime and seen a getaway car. They can't remember the full plate but they did see it, which is why they remember part of it. Hypnosis helps them see the rest of the number. You have a partial memory. If you are hypnotized again, your mind may let you complete the memory of that name you saw. If you can, it's a huge chunk of the puzzle in trying to apprehend Parker

Bennett," Sean said persuasively.

"Go ahead, honey," Frank encouraged. "Go ahead."

"Please, Eleanor," Sean said. "Dr. Papetti is away for the next ten days at a medical convention. Let me make an appointment for you for a week from Thursday. Please."

Eleanor turned and stared out at the icy waters of the Hudson River.

She looked back to Sean. "Make the appointment," she said quietly.

58

Like his boss Rudy Schell, Jonathan Pierce was passionate about finding any evidence that would lead to Parker Bennett and tie Eric Bennett to his father's crime. As an FBI agent, like Schell, Jonathan had learned to be a patient observer when he was on a surveillance job.

Like Schell, he was tall, a little over six feet. Unlike Schell, Jonathan had a full head of dark brown hair and effortlessly kept in good physical shape. He had been a champion runner at Villanova University, which meant he could move faster than the vast majority of his fellow agents. Raised in Oyster Bay, Long Island, now a resident of Manhattan, he had an apartment in Greenwich Village and was watching with alarm as the Village lost the quaintness that had made it so special. We don't need all those celebrities gobbling up the real estate, he reminded himself from time to time.

Jonathan realized that living in the town house adjacent to the one where Anne Bennett resided was enjoyable. He liked Montclair and the people he had met there because of his supposed ownership of the new restaurant on Main Street.

However, he was watching and listening with increased alarm as Eric Bennett, on his visits every other night, told his mother that he was seeing Lane Harmon more regularly and was going to ask her to marry him.

Jonathan had Googled everything he could about Lane. He had seen the house in Georgetown where she grew up. He had found pictures of her as a little girl at the funeral of her father, Congressman Gregory Harmon. He had seen with pity the images of her with her hand on his coffin, her eyes flooded with tears, standing on the sidewalk outside the church.

He knew what schools she had attended. He had studied pictures of her with her husband, Kenneth Kurner, and reflected on how happy she looked in them.

She had lost her father in a plane crash when she was seven and her husband in a car crash when she was twenty-five and pregnant. How terrible for her, he thought. He had two healthy parents who lived on

Long Island. He had two older married brothers and six nieces and nephews.

She's an interior designer now and assistant to the famous Glady Harper. She has a four-year-old daughter, Katie. Two weeks ago Lane had posted a picture on Facebook with Katie holding her painting of the father whom she had never known.

Jon remembered the first time he had met Lane, when she came to Anne Bennett's home six weeks ago. He had seen her car turning into the driveway and rushed out to meet her. His first impression had been of her beautiful eyes and her auburn hair, the slight wind tossing it around her shoulders.

You can't fall in love with a woman by eavesdropping, he thought, and then wondered if that was happening to him. Or maybe it's because a couple of friends my age just got engaged, he tried to rationalize. Maybe turning thirty is giving all of us a jolt. Thirty-two next month, he reminded himself — who are you kidding?

Yesterday, in a call from Rudy Schell, Jon had learned that an offer was being made to give up Parker Bennett. "It's coming from that sleazebag lawyer Derek Landry," Rudy said, "and I bet one thousand to one he's representing Countess Sylvie de la Marco. We're stalling him. It grates on me to give her a free ride and a two-million-dollar reward. But I have a hunch this is coming to a head, Jon," he had concluded.

Jonathan had the same feeling. If the countess led them to Parker Bennett, they all believed the trail would lead them to Eric too. And Lane was in the thick of it.

When Eric Bennett and Lane went to dinner they were always tracked by a pair of FBI agents, a different couple every time, with a listening device on their table. But the conversations had so far yielded nothing. Lane had reassured Eric that she understood he was absolutely innocent and told him that she firmly cut off people who told her otherwise. She never revealed to him that she had been approached by the FBI.

Get rid of him, Lane, was Jonathan's constant thought. I'm worried about you.

You're going to get hurt.

59

Sylvie could not believe her luck. The two million dollars from Parker had come through and she had a date to go shopping with Barclay Cameron at Cartier. "I want to buy you an engagement ring of your choice," he told her, "and also a wedding ring. Quite frankly except for our little romance, which was after I was a widower, I have never had a physical relationship with any woman other than my wife. I was faithful to her for over fifty years. I am not comfortable in the role of being anything but a husband to you."

Sylvie's reaction was to think how charmingly naïve he was before, with genuine tears in her eyes, she said, "Oh, Barclay, yes, yes, yes."

Her next reaction was to make an appointment with another law firm, Burke & Edwards, the one that represented the de la Marco family's holdings. Then she had Robert take pictures of all the newly decorated rooms in the apartment and have them enlarged.

On Friday morning, Robert drove her to the prestigious law firm at Park Avenue and Eightieth Street. She always dressed prepared to be photographed, and if possible, even more so today. She was the Countess de la Marco. She wanted to shove that down the throat of everyone who worked at Burke & Edwards.

The importance of her visit was obvious the moment she arrived. The receptionist treated her with effusive warmth and immediately led her into a conference room where she found the three senior partners of the firm awaiting her.

They all stood when she came in. She was wearing one of her full-length Russian sables as well as carrying a sable fur muff and a small tote bag. She laid the muff on the table so that no one missed it. She thought that it added a little glamour. Countesses in the nineteenth century had all carried them.

Then she reached into the tote bag and came right to the point. "According to the prenuptial agreement you prepared and I signed with my beloved husband Eduardo, besides the modest sum of money I received upon his death, I am entitled to lifelong use of my apartment including its maintenance unless I remarry."

"That is correct, Countess," the senior partner, Clinton Chambers, confirmed.

"I will lay my cards on the table," Sylvie said. "I have a gentleman whose name you would recognize who cares deeply about me. He would like to marry me or live with me. It is my choice. If I decide to live with him, you will be paying the maintenance of the apartment and no one in the family will have use of it until I die. I assure you I am in very good health. My parents are still alive and both of my grandmothers lived past ninety-five." She paused and smiled. "I know that apartment was purchased fifty years ago for two hundred fifty thousand dollars, which of course is an incredibly low figure by today's standards. It's now worth close to twenty million dollars because of its size and location."

She opened the tote bag. "I have recently undertaken a large redecoration and some minor renovation of the apartment by the famed interior designer Glady Harper. I would like you to pass these enlarged pictures around. As you can see the apartment is now in pristine condition and exquisitely furnished."

She waited as they passed the photographs around. Clinton Chambers said, "You are right, Countess, the apartment is very beautiful. What do you want from us?"

"I want you to buy from me my legal interest in the apartment at the bargain price of ten million plus the five million I spent for the recent redecorating. You all know that buyers will scramble to take it off your hands for far more than that or you can rent it for an exorbitant fee."

"Those are hardly the terms of your prenup agreement, Countess," Chambers said frostily.

Sylvie said, "They may not be, but the de la Marcos are salivating to get that apartment and you know it. Eduardo had three sons and two daughters. I only knew them slightly but I can guarantee all five of them will fight each other for it."

She stood up. "I want my answer in forty-eight hours. When I have it, I will be out of the apartment in twenty-four hours, but of course, I will be carrying a certified check for fifteen million dollars in my hand."

She could see how reluctantly the three partners got to their feet. "Just remember," she said, "I have no problem at all being a fiancée, until death do us part."

Robert was waiting downstairs at the front

entrance of the building. When the doorman closed the door behind her, he said, "I
trust your meeting was pleasant, Countess."

Sylvie smiled, "Oh, I would say so. For
me, it was very pleasant."

60

After the meeting at Rudy Schell's office Lane and Glady were frosty to each other for two days. Then Glady said, "Lane, I'm going to do something I hate to do, and that is to apologize. We don't have to discuss what we don't agree about, but I promise I will not make a negative remark in your presence about Eric Bennett. Is it a deal?"

"Yes, Glady, thank you."

But even though she had made peace with Glady, Lane was not at peace with herself. She realized how confused she was about Eric. It's not so much about his guilt or innocence, she admitted to herself. I *know* he's innocent. It's about my feelings toward him.

As she had expected, Eric was no longer satisfied with seeing her once a week. "Lane, we can go out to dinner in the city after Katie's asleep," he pointed out. "Wouldn't your babysitter be happy to make a few extra dollars? She lives right in your building, doesn't she? If we had dinner at nine o'clock, you'd be home by eleven o'clock."

He'd asked to see Katie again. "I'd like to spend a Saturday or Sunday with the *two* of you," he said. "The Christmas show at Radio City is opening. You tell me that Katie is a good skater. Have you ever taken her to the rink in Rockefeller Plaza?"

In one of their conversations she had told him that when she was a child, she used to go skating with her father. "My dad was a natural and so is Katie."

Eric told her that his mother would like her to visit. "Maybe on Saturday, instead of meeting me at the restaurant, you could come a little earlier and spend some time with her?"

Eric was persuasive and charming. He was starting to bring her little gifts — not too expensive, but thoughtful, caring, well chosen.

The last one was a Montblanc pen with her initials engraved on it. When he gave it to her he said, "I can't believe that I saw you take out that cheap throwaway when you rummaged in your purse for your cell phone."

"I had a good one, but I lost it somewhere and never got around to replacing it," she told him. "That's so sweet of you to notice."

But the question that persistently hammered at her was, why did Dwight hate him so much? She knew her feelings about Dwight had changed during Thanksgiving weekend, but why did Dwight hate him so much?

There had been another item, this time in Cindy Adams's column in the *Post,* about Eric and her enjoying a tête-à-tête at Primola on Second Avenue in Manhattan.

But at least the Fifth Avenue apartment of Countess Sylvie de la Marco was almost complete now except for a few throw pillows, some semivaluable bric-a-brac, deliveries of end tables, and new bedspreads in the guest bedrooms. Glady had told her this morning that the two million from the countess finally arrived.

Though Glady and she never talked about it, Lane was uncomfortable to know that there were listening devices in de la Marco's home.

She had come to like the countess. It was amusing to watch the way she went from the veneer of nobility to her roots in a lower-middle-class family.

When Glady was around the countess stayed in the library, but when Lane was there alone she often stopped in to chat with her. When she commented on some of the artwork Glady had ordered, she said, "Lane, if this stuff is going to be worth ten times what I paid for it, the world is going nuts. It looks like finger painting to me."

Lane thought it better to not tell the countess that she agreed with her.

That evening she met Eric for one of their Tuesday night dinners in Manhattan. He said, "Lane, my mother's birthday is Thursday. She refuses to go out for dinner, but she would love it if you would come see her again. We'll toast her over a glass of wine, then go out to dinner ourselves."

Lane had visited Anne the last two Saturdays. She truly liked her, but Anne too had been pressing her to bring Katie out for a visit. Tuesday and Saturday for dinner and now Thursday? It's too much, she thought. It's way too much.

But because it was Anne's birthday, she reluctantly agreed. When she accepted the offer, she knew there was something she had to do. She was going to call Dwight and plead with him to tell her why he despised Eric Bennett.

61

On Wednesday afternoon, carrying his bags, Parker Bennett left the Day and Night Motel for the last time.

He hailed a cab and instructed the driver to take him to the Miami Amtrak station. He had known he was in plenty of time for the afternoon train to Newark, but he still couldn't stand the thought that he might be caught in some unexpected traffic jam. And he hated the idea of the twenty-six-and-a-half-hour trip.

On the way, he reviewed everything that had happened these last few weeks. He hadn't been answering Sylvie's calls, but she had left a message, "Parker, you have five billion dollars. You've given me nice gifts over these two years, but they're a drop in the bucket compared to what you're sitting on. I have to finish paying the decorator now."

The last sentence had clearly been an

outright threat.

In the hope of buying time, he had sent her the two million dollars she demanded, but he knew that would not buy her silence if she thought he was about to be caught. He hadn't dared to refuse her, but after he bought the villa in Switzerland he only had five thousand dollars left. And he still had to buy his airline ticket to Switzerland.

After two weeks at the Night and Day Motel, he tried to take comfort in the fact that he was unrecognizable as either Parker Bennett or George Hawkins.

Posing as an actor, he had gone to a theatrical supply house. Terrified that the clerk would recognize him when he took off the brown wig, he had quickly bought two others, one gray with a ponytail and one salt and pepper, long enough to cover his ears.

His beard had come in. As he'd expected, it was gray with a sprinkling of white. He had put on ten pounds and they emphasized the jowls on his chin, but he was desperate. He was almost out of money.

He had to hope that even if that loudmouth Len decided to turn him in, he hadn't done it yet.

"Hey, mister, do you want to get out?"

Startled, Parker looked up and then realized the taxi had arrived at the Miami Amtrak station. "Oh, of course, daydreaming I guess."

After paying the fare he got out of the cab. Dragging his suitcases, he went up to the ticket counter. "One way on the four o'clock train to Newark, a sleeper car, please."

"Yes, sir. That will get into Newark at six-thirty P.M. tomorrow. How would you like to pay for that?"

"With cash."

"Please let me see your ID."

He knew she was scrutinizing him carefully. "As you can see, I've gotten honest with my hair. I stopped dyeing it," he said, trying to laugh.

She smiled and said, "That will be nine hundred seventy-five dollars."

So far, so good, he thought, as he headed toward his gate. She did not react to the George Hawkins ID. And taking Amtrak solved another problem. He knew he would have been taking a huge chance if he had tried to bring the handgun he had purchased on a plane. But Amtrak does not screen luggage and carry-ons.

I only have to use the George Hawkins ID twice more, he thought, for the rental car and the flight to Geneva. His Swiss contact, Adolph, had assured him that when he got to Switzerland, in exchange for an enormous fee, a new identity would be awaiting him.

Three hours before reaching Newark he phoned Swissair and asked if there were seats available on that evening's Geneva flight. "It's wide open, sir. Can I make a reservation for you?"

"No, thanks. I'll buy my ticket tonight."

On his iPhone he found an Enterprise rental near the Newark train station. He phoned and reserved a car. He would pick it up at seven thirty P.M. That would get him to Anne's town house at about eight P.M. He had gone online and done a virtual tour of the street where her town house was located. Cars were parked on it but it was never filled.

It was Anne's birthday. That meant she would be in her town house. In her peculiarly stubborn way she just wouldn't go out on birthdays or holidays.

He was counting on the fact that she would still have the music box. If for any reason the music box was gone, it was all over. But she had told him that of all the many gifts he had given her, this was her favorite. He was counting on the fact that she would never dispose of it.

Suppose Eric happened to be with her? It was an eventuality he had to face; somehow, he would have to deal with it.

The eleven P.M. flight from Newark to Geneva. He had to be on it.

After he got the number from the music box, he would make an excuse to leave Anne for a few hours, drive to Newark airport, and buy the ticket to Geneva. He'd pay for it in cash.

He had renewed the George Hawkins British passport once in the last thirteen years. Surely no security screener would pay much notice if his hair was no longer brown but gray, and worn a little longer.

The danger was that if either Sylvie or Len had turned him in, they would definitely be watching for Parker Bennett/George Hawkins at the airports.

62

On Thursday afternoon a bored Len Stacey stared out the window of his home in St. Thomas. It was raining again, which meant there would be no golf today, and possibly tomorrow.

Never interested in reading and having nothing to do, he once again began to think of his friend George Hawkins, who so resembled the pictures in the newspapers of Parker Bennett, the Wall Streeter who took off with all that money. "And when I yelled, 'Parker,' he spun around," he told his wife for the tenth or twentieth time.

Finally, her patience snapped. "Len, this is eating you up. I'm tired of telling you to call the FBI in New York. You can tell them that you're probably way off base but you think that what's his name, George Hawkins, may be that crook. There's a reward out for anyone who finds him, isn't there?"

"A two-million-dollar reward, but suppose I'm wrong and George ever heard about it? I'd feel bad."

Not for the first time since her husband of forty years had tried her patience to the snapping point, Barbara wanted to scream "Shut up" at him. Now, gritting her teeth, she said, "Len, I want you to call the FBI. And then no matter if you get a reward or they tell you to go fly a kite, I do not want to hear the name George Hawkins again so long as I live!"

Her voice escalating, she stared at him. "Do you get that, Len? Do you *get* it?"

Len Stacey escaped her withering glance, mumbling, "Maybe I will call. Let me think about it."

63

On Thursday afternoon Sylvie and Barclay Cameron were led to a quiet room in Cartier and seated at a mahogany table.

Barclay told her he had selected three different engagement rings and three different wedding bands for her to choose from.

Sylvie could see that he was the picture of happiness. And to think I got involved with Parker instead of hanging on to him, she thought. What was the matter with me?

Her satisfaction from her meeting with the de la Marco lawyers was beginning to dissipate. What good would all of this do if Parker was found and turned her in?

The manager returned with a black velvet tray. The rings Barclay had selected were on it. One of the engagement rings was a large square diamond surrounded by emeralds. The second one was an equally large oval diamond edged by sapphires.

Two of the engagement rings were brilliant diamonds. The third was a breathtakingly large yellow diamond that had not as yet been set.

The Cartier manager pointed out how flawless all the diamonds were and that the yellow diamond was very rare, large, and unblemished.

The wedding rings were diamond bands in three different widths.

Sylvie knew that the yellow diamond was by far the most valuable.

"Now perhaps all of these are too showy. Perhaps you would enjoy smaller stones," Barclay said.

Sylvie heard the teasing note in his voice. "Guess which one I want?" she challenged him.

"The yellow diamond and the widest wedding band," Barclay said promptly. "So be it."

"An excellent choice," the manager at Cartier said, trying to keep the excitement out of his voice.

Later, in her apartment, Sylvie's emotions swung between exultation and terror. Suppose the FBI didn't accept her offer?

Suppose they caught Parker and he told them about sending her money? Nervous and upset, she called Derek Landry.

"I want to change my offer to the FBI,"

she said. "I will not accept the reward if my information leads to Parker Bennett. If they find him and I know I'm safe from him, I will pay back every nickel he forced me to accept. I only want and demand anonymity and immunity from prosecution."

"That may change the picture," was Landry's suave response. "I will call you back, Countess."

64

At four o'clock Thursday afternoon Eleanor and Frank went to see Dr. Papetti again. Rudy Schell and Sean Cunningham were there already when they arrived. Both greeted them warmly.

As always, Sean was reassuring. "Now, Eleanor, what did I tell you?"

"That I shouldn't be nervous, that I shouldn't feel as though I'm letting you down if I don't remember George somebody's last name." She managed to smile even while she clutched Frank's hand.

Dr. Papetti was waiting for her when they were escorted into his office. "I'm glad you've come back, Eleanor," he said. "I understand it's been a hard decision for you to make."

"It was, but just in case I may be able to help by doing it, I'll take my ride in the elevator again."

Without waiting for an answer she walked

350

over to the La-Z-Boy, sat down, leaned back, and closed her eyes.

Dr. Papetti pulled up a chair beside her. "Eleanor, you are beginning a voyage you will enjoy. You are going up in an elevator. It is going to stop at every floor . . ."

Observing from across the room, Rudy Schell knew that his usual steely calm was deserting him.

If Eleanor Becker did not come up with the last name of Parker Bennett's alias, they were at a dead end; two years of fruitless investigating and still no promising leads.

And even if Eleanor remembered the last name Bennett was using, how far would it take them? They would have the assumed name and know that he has or had a British driver's license. It would be a start but there was always the chance that Bennett had other identities.

Rudy felt his cell phone vibrate and stepped out of Dr. Papetti's office and into the corridor.

It was Attorney Derek Landry. Rudy's greeting to him was curt. "Mr. Landry, we are considering your offer but —"

Landry cut him off and began speaking. As Rudy listened, he felt the hair rise on the back of his neck. Trying to sound impersonal, he asked, "Let me be clear. Your

351

client is ready to offer us Parker Bennett's alias, his current address, and phone number. And your client will forgo reward money and will pay back the value of any gifts Bennett forced upon him or her. In return we grant your client immunity from prosecution and anonymity."

"This is exactly what I am offering," Landry said.

"And I assume your client is Countess de la Marco."

"As you have already figured out, yes, she is."

"Mr. Landry, I have your number. I'll call you right back."

From the Contacts list on his phone, Rudy pressed the number of Milton Harsh, the assistant United States attorney handling the case.

Less than one minute later Harsh said, "Rudy, take the deal!"

Rudy called Landry, who answered on the first ring. "Mr. Landry, we agree to your client's terms."

"Excellent," Landry exclaimed. "When will you be back in your office, Mr. Schell?"

"In half an hour."

Rudy went back into Dr. Papetti's office in time to hear Eleanor say, "His name is George Hawkins."

65

Thirty minutes later, Rudy Schell was in the office. Derek Landry arrived close behind him.

"I have a legal agreement outlining the terms we discussed for you to sign, and I have the information you need on Parker Bennett," Landry said smiling. "My client is so happy to be of assistance to you. As I have explained, Countess Sylvie de la Marco can give you Parker Bennett's alias, address, and phone number."

Landry continued. "My client will return the value of any gifts that were forced upon her and —"

Rudy interrupted. "Mr. Landry, give me the information on Parker Bennett."

He almost grabbed the sheet from Landry's hand, perused it, and returned his gaze to Landry.

"And there is the matter of our legal agreement," Landry said, as he pushed it across the table.

Rudy quickly reviewed it and then scrawled his signature on it. As he handed it back he thought about how much he hated doing this, that the countess should go to prison, but reminded himself that he had no choice but to sign it.

Thanks to Eleanor they believed they knew Bennett's other identity and that he most likely had a British passport, but that was all. George Hawkins was a common name in Britain. Now we're getting close to the whole picture, Rudy thought.

66

As soon as Derek Landry was escorted to the door, the immense capacity of the FBI to take instant action was set in motion. When Rudy Schell provided the cell phone number of Parker Bennett, alias George Hawkins, in approximately thirty minutes the agents were able to pinpoint his exact location on the Amtrak train. They listened as he made a phone call to reserve a White Honda Accord at Newark Penn Station. Two hours later, when Bennett got off the train, a swarm of agents was watching him as the Honda was delivered.

The surveillance team had two cars ready to follow him and two more positioned in front of him. A helicopter hovered overhead as insurance.

As lead investigator on the Bennett case for two years, Rudy Schell was in one of the cars. "I think he's going to his wife's house," he told the others. "Otherwise, why go to

New Jersey? Jon Pierce is recording every word that is spoken there. We want to hear what he tells his wife. If we get them together we might find out if she and the son are involved. We'll close in on him if he makes any attempt to leave."

But the thought crossed his mind: Is it just possible he's too clever for us? Bennett had to know it was risky to return to the area and make contact with his wife and son. The question is, why is he doing this?

67

It was her birthday. Anne was so glad that Lane had agreed to stop in with Eric and pay her a visit before they went out to dinner. Eric had tried to convince her to join them, but as he should have expected, no amount of persuasion would make Anne do that.

Birthdays and holidays are meant to be spent at home, she thought, and besides, I just don't feel well.

Her newfound sense of peace in the town house had subsided. Of course she loved it. It was so pretty and the size was exactly right for her. She loved the living room and remembered how Lane had said that it was lacking something. A week later the throw pillows Lane had ordered had arrived and the warmth of the colors had perfectly complemented the couch and wing chair. Anne could not have been happier with the completed look.

How very dear Lane is, she thought. How sweet it was of her to have stopped in on these last few Saturdays to visit me. But the one thing Anne would never discuss with Lane, or, for that matter, with Eric, was that she missed her husband. Even as a young woman, when she had married Parker, she had known she would not be getting a faithful husband. She was only twenty-two at the time but she could remember hearing other women who worked in the office speak so adoringly about Parker and how charming he could be. Anne knew perfectly well what they were saying.

But she also had always known that there was something in him that needed her unquestioning loyalty. She so desperately wanted to believe that something in his head had made him unaware of what he was doing when he had cheated all those people.

And she was so worried about Eric. She wanted to believe that he had no part in it, but she wasn't sure. On top of all of that, she really didn't feel well. The Christmas tree Eric had brought in two days ago — a full-branched tree at her request — had yet to be decorated. At dinner the other night Eric had strung the bulbs and brought down from the storage room the boxes of ornaments and unused tinsel. Anne had planned to trim the tree this evening, but now, with the nagging pain in her left arm, she would wait until tomorrow.

At seven o'clock Eric pulled into the driveway. Ten minutes later Lane's car pulled up behind his. Lane had bought a Christmas wreath for the front door of the town house; the aroma of fresh pine and holly permeated the air.

"You look so pretty, Lane," Anne exclaimed as Lane kissed her hello.

Lane was wearing an emerald-green silk blouse with long sleeves and tailored black slacks. She had a single strand of white pearls around her neck. She had worn them on her last visit and had told Anne that they were an engagement present from her mother, that they had belonged to Lane's grandmother.

"That emerald green is so perfect with your auburn hair," Anne said.

Anne did not realize that Lane was looking at her with increasing alarm. Lane saw that Anne's complexion was deathly pale. She had faint beads of perspiration on her forehead and she was moving very slowly. She seemed almost unsteady on her feet.

When she had called Dwight to ask him to tell her the reason for his brutal criticism of Eric, he had said, "Lane, I want to tell

359

you but first I need to be released from a promise I made. I'll call you back." Lane felt almost like a betrayer now that she saw the expression in Anne's eyes and realized how glad Anne was to see her. Spotting the Christmas tree gave Lane a chance to avoid any conversation that might become too personal.

"Oh, Anne," she said. "Would you accept any help in decorating your tree? I am really good at it, even if I do say so myself. You could never reach those higher branches. I'll ask Eric to give me a hand. I can instruct him on where to place the ornaments."

"My mother always insisted on getting out the stepladder and doing it herself," Eric said. "I think that's a great idea, Lane. How about it, Mom?"

"Oh, Lane, that would be lovely," Anne replied happily. "I do so want to see my tree decorated but I wasn't looking forward to the task. Eric, are you sure? I know you have a dinner reservation."

"I've been trying to help you put the tree up practically since I was born," he laughed. "Lane, tell me what to do first."

Anne watched them, delighted, and in less than half an hour the tree was sparkling with the ornaments and multicolored lights and the tinsel was glittering on the branches.

Then Lane pulled the crèche out of the last storage box.

"Oh, this is beautiful," she exclaimed.

"My father made it," Anne said. "He hand-carved every piece in it. The cradle, the figures of the Christ child and Mary and Joseph, and the shepherds and the angels and the livestock. Every single piece."

She looked at Eric.

"Your father never appreciated what a skilled craftsman your grandfather was. I don't think you did either."

Eric smiled but did not respond.

A few minutes later Lane restacked the empty boxes and asked Eric to put them away. When he had left the room, Anne got up and reached for the music box that was on the mantel over the fireplace.

"Lane," she said slowly. "The first year we were married my husband gave me this for my birthday. When you turn the key it plays 'The Song Is Ended (but the Melody Lingers On).' I listen to it frequently but it's particularly meaningful to me on my birthday."

As she lifted the music box off the mantel, it slipped through her fingers and smashed against the bricks of the raised fireplace. The dancing figures and the velvet cushion they had been placed on tumbled out just as Eric came running back into the room.

"What happened?" he asked, alarmed.

Before Anne could answer, Eric's eyes rested on the broken music box.

"I'll buy another one for you, Mother," he said softly. Before he could pick up the box, it was already in Anne's hand.

A small strip of paper was taped to the inside of the box. Puzzled, Anne studied it. "There's a number on this paper," she said. "I guess it's the design number."

Almost too quickly, Eric snatched the music box from her hand.

"Let me see that."

Lane watched him as an expression she found hard to interpret came over his face. He carefully peeled the paper from the side of the box, opened his wallet, and placed it inside.

"No, Mother, it's the scrial number. And whether you like it or not, I'm going to get you a new music box."

That's not the serial number, Lane thought. The serial number is never taped inside. If there is one, it's engraved on the bottom of thc box.

The cylinder had not been broken. Anne wound the box and waited. The song began to play.

"As long as it still plays our song," she

said. "It doesn't matter if it's broken." Tears in her eyes, Anne Bennett began to softly sing, "But the melody lingers on."

68

Ranger had been waiting outside Eric Bennett's office building at five P.M. on Thursday. He knew the time had come. He couldn't wait any longer. Maybe he wouldn't kill the mother. He had followed her to Mass again on Sunday and seen how frail she looked. Maybe he'd just shoot Eric and be done with it. He'd do it just when Eric turned into his apartment building.

But tonight, when he followed Eric, he went directly to his garage. Ranger then followed him to Anne Bennett's town house.

The fact that Christmas trees were lighted with colorful bulbs on the lawns all over Montclair made everything that much worse.

Everyone in the world had someone and he was alone.

Alone, alone, alone . . .

Judy, Judy, Judy . . .

The voices were clamoring in his head.

Kill them, kill them, kill them . . . The heater in the car had stopped working and it was as cold inside as it was outside.

His fingers were stiff. He remembered how after he had bathed and fed her, Judy would slip her fingers into his and tell him how good he was to her and how much she loved him.

Then a car drove past him and parked behind Eric's in the driveway. It was the girlfriend. This was his chance. The three of them were inside that house. But suddenly nervous, Ranger could not force himself to leave the car. He was starting to hear Judy's voice again.

About half an hour later, Eric and the girlfriend came out again and got into their cars. They're probably going to a restaurant.

Habit made Ranger follow them.

69

He was almost there. Parker Bennett, his throat agonizingly dry, drove in light traffic to Montclair. He had not been in New Jersey very often, but the navigation system made it easy. When he turned off the highway into Montclair he became aware of the charm of the Christmas lights on so many of the lawns.

Professional decorators had handled the Christmas decorations both inside and outside of the Greenwich mansion. A string of cars had driven by to see and admire the splendid display. Anne, being Anne, had always put up a tree in her sitting room and decorated it herself with the lights and ornaments she had taken from her old home after her parents died. She also had a crèche under the tree. There wasn't a year she had missed.

Parker was sure she had the same display in her new home.

He reflected on the events of the past two years. The Fund had stopped growing. It had become impossible to keep the auditors at bay. The SEC was closing in. It was time to go. Immediately.

He had always felt secure knowing that at any time he could step into his new life as George Hawkins. On the other hand, he had begun to mistrust Eric. He had been almost certain that Eric was planning to cheat him. That was why he had switched most of the money into the second account.

He had carefully planned his escape. He had stored the small inflatable dinghy and the outboard motor George Hawkins had bought in the well of his large sailboat in St. John. His exit strategy was to abandon the sailboat on the open water and take the dinghy to St. Thomas. Over the years he had practiced the best route to take. The planning had paid off.

It was a long trip in choppy seas. Six hours after Parker Bennett abandoned ship off Tortola, George Hawkins steered the dinghy into the dock outside his small villa in St. Thomas.

"You will reach your destination in five hundred feet on the right," the electronic voice of the navigation system reported.

Unaware that he was being observed not

only by Ranger but by a dozen FBI agents, Parker got out of his car, walked up to the front door of the town house, took out his phone, and dialed Anne's number.

He had not heard her voice in two years but immediately discerned how different it sounded — low and tired.

"Anne," he said, "it's me. I'm at the door. I can't stay away from you any longer. I'm going to turn myself in but first I need to spend a few hours with you."

Anne was gasping. "Oh, Parker, is it really you? Am I dreaming?"

"Anne, let me in." The connection broke. Less than twenty seconds later Parker heard the sound of the latch being turned, and the door opened. He stepped inside, closed it, put his arms around Anne, and embraced her tightly.

She was crying. "I knew you'd come back to me. I knew it."

His arm around her, he walked with her into the living room.

"I almost expected to hear your music box playing. Where is it?" he asked, trying not to sound too eager.

And then he spotted it on the cocktail table, open, the broken figures beside it.

"I dropped it twenty minutes ago," Anne said, "but it still plays our song. Isn't that wonderful?" She looked directly at him. "Oh, Parker, you look so different, but I know you've had to hide yourself."

"Anne, there was a piece of paper here inside the box. Where is it?" Bennett's voice had lost any hint of tenderness.

"Eric put it in his wallet."

"Where is he?"

Suddenly frightened and bewildered, Anne Bennett stared at her husband. "Eric went out to dinner."

"Is he going straight home?"

"No, he said he was going to stop in on me before he goes back to New York. Oh, Parker, he's so angry at you. You can understand that."

Parker Bennett nodded. "I can understand that. I want to make peace with Eric as well, if that's possible. Now, Anne, let's sit together until he gets here . . ."

"Oh, yes, yes."

"And let's play our song."

He picked up the music box, wound it up, and listened as Anne, in a trembling but sweet voice, sang, "The song is ended but the melody lingers on."

70

There's something different about Eric, Lane realized. He seemed to be so utterly engaged with his own thoughts that her attempts at conversation were futile. It was as though he was not listening to anything she said.

As they waited for the entrée to be served, he gulped rather than sipped his wine and even began drumming his fingers on the table.

For all the world she felt that he was merely going through the motions of dinner and anxious to have it over with. He certainly was not the charming man she had been seeing these last six weeks. He had lied to his mother when he said the paper taped inside the music box was a serial number. What possible reason could he have had for that?

But more importantly, she was concerned about Anne Bennett. Doesn't he realize that his mother may be very ill?

"Eric, has your mother ever had any heart trouble?" she asked.

"What? Oh, some. She can get an irregular heartbeat but that hasn't happened since right after my father disappeared."

Lane always had her phone in her pocket set on vibrate in case she received a call from home about Katie. She felt it go off now. "Oh, sorry," she said. She glanced at the phone and could see the name of the caller. It was Dwight Crowley, her stepfather. Quickly, she disconnected.

"Who was that?" Eric asked.

Lane thought quickly and then with a smile in her voice said, "It was my dear employer, Glady Harper, who thinks nothing of calling me any time between seven A.M. and midnight if there's something she wants to tell me."

Eric nodded, not so much as though he understood but as though he was either disinterested or simply not focused.

"Eric, you didn't even hear me," Lane said. "I think you're almost paralyzed with worry, and I think you have every reason to be concerned about your mother. Why don't you give her a call?"

A hint of annoyance came over Eric's face. "Lane, you're very solicitous about my mother and I appreciate that but she doesn't look much different today than she did yesterday and the day before that. But if it will make you happy . . ."

He picked up his cell phone and pressed her number. It rang five times and then the answering machine, with its electronic voice, came on.

"Maybe she went to bed," he said.

"And maybe she didn't," Lane snapped. "Eric, your mother is sick. Let's go back right now."

Eric hesitated, stood up, and then said, "Maybe you're right. You stay here. I can be back in fifteen minutes."

"I'm coming with you," Lane said firmly.

Shrugging, Eric threw a one-hundred-dollar bill on the table. "If you insist," he said as the waiter, entrées in his hand, stared at them.

71

They went into a restaurant about five minutes away. It was the one they had gone into the first time Ranger had followed them. Ranger parked his car and once again got a table across the room from them. But then just as their dinner came, Eric threw money on the table and they both rushed out.

Without bothering to pay his bill, acting as if he was going to the bathroom, Ranger followed them, then ducked out the front door of the restaurant behind them.

While Eric and Lane gave their tickets to the valet, Ranger hustled across the street to where he had parked. He followed their cars back to the town house. He figured something had to be wrong inside because of the way they were rushing.

He watched Eric run out of the car, the girlfriend a step behind him.

He might not have this chance again. All

three of them. Why not? The voices were screaming at him, "Now! Now! Now!"

Ranger reached into the backseat for the package he would carry as an excuse to ring the doorbell and get into the house.

And then it would be over.

72

When Anne's phone rang, Parker Bennett looked at the name of the caller and then let the phone ring until he heard the voice of his son inquiring anxiously, "Mom, are you okay? Mom, I know you're there. Pick up the phone."

When Anne went to take it out of his hand, Parker held it away from her until the connection broke.

"Anne, listen to me," he said. "Before I turn myself in, I have to make my peace with my son. In his state of mind, if he knew I was here, he might very well call the FBI."

"Oh, Parker," Anne said. "I didn't think of that. I do need to have you and Eric make peace before I die."

For the first time Bennett looked closely at his wife and saw how ghostly pale she was and the slight beads of perspiration that had formed on her forehead.

Filled with genuine concern, he asked,

"Anne, have you had your heart checked recently? You don't look as if you feel well."

Anne shook her head and moved closer to her husband on the sofa. "Oh yes, I do take my heart medicine but some days I'm just not feeling quite right and this is one of them."

She looked up at him. "Parker, let me look at you as you are. That must be a wig. Take it off. And please don't turn yourself in until tomorrow. Give me one last night with you."

She leaned her head on his shoulder. "I love you," she said. "I am so desperately sorry for the people whose money you took but it can't be all gone. Can you just leave it where it will be found and can we hide somewhere? I just want to be with you for the rest of my life."

Parker Bennett had a moment of deep regret for the life he had chosen.

But then he pictured himself in his new villa in Switzerland and the life of luxury he'd be heading for once he got on that plane tonight.

73

The dozen members of the FBI surveillance team, now surrounding the town house, were listening to the tense reports that Jonathan Pierce was giving them.

Jon watched as Lane and Eric ran into the town house where Parker Bennett was waiting. Jon knew the situation might be explosive and told Rudy Schell that. But Rudy answered sharply, "We don't know yet if both of them were involved. We have to hear what they say to each other."

"And there's an old black Ford sedan parked down the block with an older white male driver inside. It looks as though he might have been following them. It may be the same car you saw following Anne Bennett. We're watching it."

74

When Lane and Eric rushed into the living room Anne was slumped on the couch, her eyes closed. Lane dropped to her knees beside Anne, reached for her wrist, then cried, "Eric, I can't get a pulse. She's not breathing. Call nine-one-one." But even as she spoke, she knew that Anne was dead.

Eric pulled out his cell phone. Then a voice from the doorway said, "That can wait. Hello, Eric."

Lane dropped her fingers from Anne Bennett's wrist and stood up. She had seen so many pictures of Parker Bennett in the newspapers. There was no mistaking the man. It was Parker Bennett. And then what she heard shocked her.

"You have the number, Eric. Give it to me."

The number that was taped in the music box! Lane thought. What does it mean?

"I don't think that's possible, Dad," Eric

said, his voice smooth and unemotional. "Now, for Mother's sake, get out of here. I don't want you to be arrested. You must have a fallback plan, whatever it is, to hide somewhere. Let that be the end of it."

You can't do that, Eric, Lane thought. You have got to turn him in.

Then in horror she watched as Parker Bennett took his hand out of his pocket and pointed a pistol at his son.

"What do you think you're doing, Dad?" Eric Bennett asked as he looked at the gun.

"What I'm doing is telling you to throw your wallet over to me. Your mother said that you put the number I want in it."

When Eric did not reply, Parker said, "Eric, I know what you are thinking, but I didn't cheat you. I was planning to share the money with you."

"How do you define cheating?" Eric asked. "You took off without telling me. I did everything you asked me to do for thirteen years. You would have been caught immediately if I hadn't put together and run the system that generated the client statements. You took almost all of the money we were supposed to share out of our account. The little that was left there I didn't dare touch. They were watching me too closely."

"The wallet, Eric," Parker shouted.

Eric pulled his wallet from his pocket and flipped it toward Parker. As his father reached to catch it, Eric hurled himself across the room and knocked him down.

The pistol went off twice, wounding Eric in his right arm and shoulder. As Lane watched unbelieving, Eric grabbed his father's hand and turned the gun on him. Parker Bennett screamed, "Don't, don't, please."

Eric said, "Bye, bye, Daddy," and pulled the trigger.

The bullet went squarely between Parker Bennett's eyes. His blood mingled with Eric's as he gasped and died.

Eric struggled to his feet, stared at Lane, and smiled. It was as though his face had been transformed. His eyes were narrow dark pits. His smile was a sneer. Supporting his wounded right arm with his left hand, he pointed the gun at Lane.

"I'm sorry, Lane. I was starting to like you. But just to let you know, I'm glad that swine shot me. Now everyone will believe I am innocent and I will have the five billion dollars I earned over thirteen years. My father's fingerprints as well as mine are on the gun. They'll believe me when I tell them he shot me, he killed you, and then himself."

His finger began to tighten on the trigger.

"I promise I'll visit Katie. I'll dry her tears. Maybe she'll make more cookies for me."

75

The instant he heard the sound of gunfire, Jonathan Pierce was out the door, running across the driveway and onto the steps of Anne Bennett's home, knowing it might already be too late to save Lane. He shot the lock open and, with a thrust of his shoulder, broke into the town house and ran into the living room. From the street, surveillance agents were pouring from their cars and were steps behind him.

76

Lane thought, Katie, Katie, I can't leave her.

Instinctively, she threw herself to the side and then felt a searing pain in her forehead. Blood began pouring down her face. She looked around wildly.

Then, before Eric could fire again, she grabbed the music box off the cocktail table and threw it at him, hitting him in the wounded shoulder.

With a cry of pain, he dropped the pistol. Snarling, he reached down, grabbed it, stood up, and aimed again at Lane.

As he ran toward the living room Jonathan was terrified that it might be too late. Eric was pointing the gun at Lane. Fearing he might hit Lane, Jon could not fire. He hurled himself across the room and collided with Eric, knocking him to the floor. In a final irony the bullet intended for Lane came to rest inside the shattered music box.

Rudy was at the head of the other FBI agents who were pouring into the room. As they surrounded Eric Bennett, Jon looked heartsick as Lane crumpled to the floor.

"Lane, Lane," he shouted as he dropped to his knees beside her and put his arms around her.

Rudy Schell was alongside him. As he wiped the blood from Lane's forehead, Jon said numbly, "I don't think the bullet went through her head. I saw it. I think she moved just in time."

Lane could hear his voice as if from a long distance away. Dear God, I am not going to die, she thought. I am not going to die. Profound gratitude was the last emotion she felt before she woke up in the hospital and looked into the eyes of the man who saved her life.

77

Ranger heard the shots and wondered if they were real or if he was hearing them in his head. He was seated in the car staring numbly ahead. The package that he planned to use as an excuse for someone to let him into Anne Bennett's town house was on the seat beside him. The pistol was on the floor in front of the passenger seat.

He heard a shout: "Put your hands on top of the steering wheel. Now come out with your hands up."

Ranger barely heard the voice because he was hearing another voice in his head. As the doors of the car were yanked open, he looked up. "It's all right," he said. "Judy wouldn't let me kill them."

78

On Friday morning Len Stacey made the call to the FBI. When he was connected, he cleared his throat and said, "I may have some very valuable information for you about Parker Bennett. If I'm right, I can tell you where he's been living, where he's going, and his cell phone number.

"I understand there is a two-million-dollar reward if my information leads to his capture."

"I'm afraid you're twenty-four hours too late, Mr. Stacey," he was told. "Read today's newspapers. Parker Bennett died last night."

"You mean I was right? You mean, he was using the name George Hawkins?"

"Yes, he was. Thank you, Mr. Stacey. Good-bye."

Len heard the click. I was right, he thought. And if I'd called the minute I suspected him, I would have the two-million-dollar reward.

He decided there was no point in telling his wife. She had told him never to talk about Parker Bennett/George Hawkins again.

79

A week later they were gathered in Rudy Schell's office. Lane, Glady, Eleanor and Frank Becker, Sean Cunningham, and Jonathan Pierce.

"I want to inform you of all the further developments in the case," Rudy said.

"Mr. and Mrs. Becker, let's start with you. Eric Bennett has said that in no way were you involved in the fraud. He has admitted that he and his father joked about how naïve you were and that the warmth and hospitality you showed to potential clients was a great help in winning their trust. He confirmed that you were absolutely unaware of any impropriety at the Parker Bennett Investment Fund. I can assure you that with the information we have given to the federal prosecutor, the charges against you will be dropped."

Eleanor gasped and turned to her husband. "Frank, I'm not going to prison.

I'm not going to prison."

Rudy turned to Glady. "Ms. Harper, I want to tell you how grateful we are for your cooperation."

"Well, have you been able to nail the countess? We all know she was in on it," Glady asked in her usual tart voice.

"We are not planning to charge the countess with any wrongdoing," Rudy said smoothly. "I can't say anything more than that."

"That's too bad. I'd have sworn she was in cahoots with him, and with all the work we did on that apartment, leave it to her to move out just when it's finished."

"What will happen to Ranger?" Sean Cunningham asked quietly.

"He agreed to get inpatient psychiatric care," Rudy said.

"Will he be charged with carrying an unlicensed pistol?"

"Probably, but I believe, considering all the circumstances, he will only get probation."

Lane had been listening quietly. In this past week the wound on her forehead had faded even though the doctor told her there would always be a small scar there. In the two days she had spent in the hospital, her mother and Dwight had flown up to be with

389

her and take care of Katie. When Dwight had tried to phone her during the dinner with Eric, he had been going to tell her that his cousin Regina Crowley Fitzsimmons had released him from the vow he made to her mother that he would never tell anyone what Eric had done to her.

Everyone told me I was wrong about Eric, Lane thought. How could I have been so stubborn? The old adage that "there are none so blind as those who will not see" kept recurring in her mind.

Now Rudy Schell turned to her. "Ms. Harmon, you were the eyewitness to what happened in Anne Bennett's home. We might have been able to arrest Eric Bennett but we would not have been able to prove that he murdered his father if you had not been there. We are confident he will serve a long term for fraud, and I can guarantee that it will be a longer term when he is also convicted of murder and attempting to murder you. He will undoubtedly spend the rest of his life in prison.

"And now the final good news — while Parker Bennett was cheating his clients, he was also making money legitimately. He did use some of his clients' money to support his lifestyle, but the great bulk of the five billion dollars has been traced and will be returned to his victims."

Jon Pierce had been sitting there quietly. Now Rudy said, "As you may know, Ms. Harmon, Agent Pierce was the one who saved your life."

Lane smiled. "I am aware of that," she said. "And all I could think of at that last moment was how terrible it would be for my daughter if I were to die."

She smiled at Jonathan, who returned the smile. Fragments of memory had come back. He had ridden with her in the back of the ambulance. His had been the first face she saw when she woke up in the hospital. She knew now that he had phoned her home and asked Mrs. Potters to stay overnight with Katie. He had contacted her mother and Dwight and told them what had happened. They had taken the next plane to New York.

When he told her his real name was Jon Pierce, not Tony Russo, she had joked that in her mind he would always be Tony. He had told her that Anthony was his middle name and some of his friends called him Tony.

He had visited her the two days she was in the hospital and he insisted that he drive her home.

When she asked him how she could ever

thank him, his reply had been, "How about dinner on Saturday night?"

She was *really* looking forward to it.

ABOUT THE AUTHOR

Mary Higgins Clark, #1 international and *New York Times* bestselling author, has written thirty-four suspense novels; three collections of short stories; a historical novel, *Mount Vernon Love Story*; two children's books, including *The Magical Christmas Horse*; and a memoir, *Kitchen Privileges*. With her daughter Carol Higgins Clark, she has coauthored five more suspense novels, and also wrote *The Cinderella Murder* with bestselling author Alafair Burke. Her books have sold more than 100 million copies in the United States alone.